BEYOND CRAZY

BEYOND CRAZY

DEB LOUGHEAD

James Lorimer & Company Ltd., Publishers
Toronto

James Lorimer & Company Ltd., Publishers acknowledges the support of the Ontario Arts Council. We acknowledge the financial support of the Government of Canada through the Canada Book Fund for our publishing activities. We acknowledge the support of the Canada Council for the Arts which last year invested $24.3 million in writing and publishing throughout Canada. We acknowledge the Government of Ontario through the Ontario Media Development Corporation's Ontario Book Initiative.

  Canadä

Cover design: Megan Fildes
Cover image: Shutterstock

Library and Archives Canada Cataloguing in Publication

Loughead, Deb, 1955-, author
     Beyond crazy / Deb Loughead.

(SideStreets)
Issued in print and electronic formats.
ISBN 978-1-4594-0717-6 (pbk.).--ISBN 978-1-4594-0718-3 (bound)
ISBN 978-1-4594-0719-0 (epub)

     I. Title. II. Series: SideStreets

PS8573.O8633B49 2014   jC813'.54   C2014-903025-8
C2014-903026-6

James Lorimer & Company Ltd.,   Distributed in the United States by:
Publishers   Orca Book Publishers
317 Adelaide Street West, Suite 1002 P.O. Box 468
Toronto, ON, Canada   Custer, WA, USA
M5V 1P9   98240-0468
www.lorimer.ca

Printed and bound in Canada.
Manufactured by Friesens Corporation in Altona, Manitoba, Canada in August 2014
Job #205574

For my 'drummer girl' niece,
Christiane Orsini

On
sta
wa

at
tie
to
of
ac
ev
fo
fr
fo

"Don't worry, Stelle. It'll all work out." She grabs my hand when I pass her, squeezes it and smiles. "You'll see, kiddo."

I so wish *she* could be my mom.

2

STUFF EVERYWHERE

I climb back through my window well after midnight. Then I sneak out of my bedroom to check on my mom, kicking junk out of the way as I go. She's asleep on the sofa. I watch the rise and fall of her chest to make sure she's still breathing. Sometimes it absolutely makes me want to cry.

My bedroom is the only space I can control, and I try to keep it neat. The kitchen, the dining room, the living room, the basement, my mom's bedroom, it's all the same. Every surface is covered with *stuff,* old magazines, newspapers, flyers, you name it. Bottles, boxes, food cartons with long-expired dates.

Before she stopped cooking and moved permanently to the sofa, I was always afraid Mom might start a fire in the kitchen. All that junk piled up on counters and on top of the stove. I've actually managed to clear it off so I can fry stuff. We keep a stash of frozen dinners and pizzas in the freezer, and canned soup, stew, and chili. And there's never *anything* fresh to eat around here if I don't do the shopping myself now and then.

My older brother, Stan, and I never ever bring anyone over to our place. I've even hidden the worst of it from Karim and Lu. I can't remember the last time they came over, and they stopped asking to visit ages ago. There's an unwritten pact between Stan and me that Mom's problem is something we'll never discuss. There's only so much you can do, only so much you can say, before you give up entirely.

Like with the whole Nana issue. I've pretty much accepted that I'm the only one who really cares about her. Mom hasn't seen her in ages. Sometimes I feel I'm the only one who has the guts to face the truth about everything that's wrong with this family.

I tuck an afghan around my mom, plant a kiss on her cheek, and head back to my room.

———

On Saturday morning the ringing doorbell wakes me up.

I drag my head out from under my pillow and peer at the clock radio. 8:00 a.m.

I burrow out from under my heap of covers and stumble from my room. Stan's bedroom door is wide open. My mom is still completely flaked out on the sofa. If she wasn't snoring I'd think she was dead. When I fling open the door, Stan is standing on the porch with his hair dishevelled and his shirt untucked. He reeks of stale smoke and beer. Cripes, he didn't even come home last night!

"Sorry," he says, shrugging. "Forgot my keys."

"You are *such* a jerk," I tell him. "Where do you go all night, anyway? Wait, I don't even want to know."

"Wasn't telling you anyway." He cackles as he sidles past, kicking stray shoes and edging around a stack of old newspapers. Then he stops in front of the sofa to stare at Mom.

"Wow. She's really starting to blend in with our décor, isn't she?" He shakes his head, then heads for his room.

I follow him down the hall, veer into the bathroom and slam the door.

"Drums? Why would you *ever* be interested in playing the *drums*, Estelle?"

My mother is standing in front of the sofa where she was sleeping just before I went to take a shower. I must have stunned her with my announcement because she's actually vertical for a change.

"Because I've always *wanted* to play them,"

I calmly try to explain. "Seriously, what's so bad about that?"

"I don't know. From what I've heard, you . . . you can get mixed up with the wrong kind of people." She won't even look me in the eye now. "It's not very promising, is it?"

"'Wrong kind of people?' Every symphony orchestra has a percussion section."

"I'd really prefer if you stick with the violin for a while, Estelle." Her voice is becoming higher with every word.

"I've been trying for a few years now and I still totally suck at it! You didn't complain when Stan quit," I tell her. "Why do you have such a problem with me?"

That shuts her up for a second. She sinks back onto the sofa.

"I *just do*, okay, Stelle?" she finally says. "So move on, will you?"

Move on? Fine. Without another word, I stomp away as dramatically as I can without tripping over something.

It's the end of the second week of September. The sun is hot on my face when I step outside early that afternoon after spending the morning sulking in my room. My tank top and shorts are plenty today.

All the way over to my dad's place, I try to figure out exactly when and how I'll break the news to my mom that I'm *already* playing the drums. That the kit is stashed at Dad and Josie's place, my sanctuary, my escape from the crazy house.

Donna, my mom, wasn't always this way. She had a pretty good job in a library after college, and married Wally. Then she played the part of the good wife and mother, working and taking care of her family at the same time. She used to read a lot, too, always had books piled up all over the house. I don't even know where those books are now — probably buried somewhere under all the trash.

But Mom never really seemed happy

underneath it all, as though a vital part of her was missing and she couldn't quite figure out what it was. She always seemed distracted, frowned a lot, didn't talk much to us or to Dad. And maybe that's why Dad's eyes and heart strayed in another direction.

It's still no excuse for bailing on us and moving in with Josie, though.

And it's no excuse for Mom to have bailed on me and Stan. Ever since the divorce, Mom just dropped out of life altogether. Never even listens to music anymore, always looks as if she's forgotten the words to her favourite song. And she started collecting all her 'stuff.' Now she's trapped under two years' worth of crap, and Stan and I are trapped with her.

Josie greets me at the door with a big grin on her wide moon face.

"Stelle! Welcome!" She hugs me and air kisses both cheeks. "Coming to practice?"

"Yeah, coming to practice," I tell her, giving her an air kiss back. She hooks her arm through mine and practically drags me inside.

This place always looks like the photos you see in those home-decorating magazines, all glossy and flawless, right down to the calla lilies in a vase on the pine harvest table, and the fresh-baked cookies cooling on the counter. She is an awesome cook, which is one thing that always makes these visits extra worthwhile.

Just as their two homes are complete opposites, so are the women who run them. Besides the fact that she's at least ten years younger than our mom, Josie is tiny and tidy. Her blonde hair and subtle makeup are always perfect. She wears designer maternity clothes, but isn't ashamed to flaunt her belly bulge with tight T-shirts.

Josie was in accounting at the insurance firm where Dad works as a salesman. After they got caught exchanging rather explicit e-mail messages, Dad confessed. When Mom threw him out, he and Josie moved in together nearby so he'd get to see me and Stan once in a while. Josie is now a freelance bookkeeper working from home. In a couple of months she's going to have a kid, a half brother or sister for me and Stan. I try my best not to think about *that*.

Dad lets me keep the drum kit he bought for me in the basement. He even built a sound-proof room so I won't disturb Josie while she's working. Stan won't set foot in Dad's house. I don't want him here anyway, finding out about the drums and ratting me out to Mom.

"Come right on in, Stelle," Josie tells me as I kick off my shoes.

"Is everything still okay for next Wednesday, when I'm bringing my friends over?" I've been putting this off for ages, but since it looks as if Josie is here to stay, they might as well meet her.

"Of course! I've got the perfect cake planned for Karim!"

"Not too healthy, I hope," I remind her. "We need a bit of decadence for Karim's sixteenth birthday shindig, right?" Josie nods and grins in a sly way.

"Thump away. There are cookies on the counter. Still warm. Your dad's out for the afternoon. He'll be sorry he missed you."

Yeah, sure he will. "Thanks, Josie," I tell her. I roll my eyes as soon as her back is turned and she's wiping the already spotless counter.

I have been hiding out in music for years. It's the best way to escape from the truth about my crazy-ass family. Chilling with Adele, and Lily Allen. Or Tegan and Sara, Mumford & Sons, and My Morning Jacket. And watching the brilliance of Hannah Ford and Meytal Cohen drumming on YouTube is epic! They're my heroes.

I started drumming with pencils or chopsticks on the kitchen table, on my desk, on my books. I drove everyone crazy with it from about age eight. That's why, once my dad left, it was easy to coerce him into buying me a kit to keep at his house. I've also been fixated on starting up a band for ages now. Sometimes just fantasizing about it takes the edge off the rest of the crap in my life.

After I pound on the drums for a while and eat a half a dozen oatmeal chocolate chip cookies, I head for home.

When I pass the plaza, kids are hovering outside the convenience store as usual. I spot a cluster of Pink Girls shuffling across the parking lot in sync like some strange giant amoeba. I always steer clear of those bimbos who seem to think that *everything* in the world is *absolutely* hilarious. *All. The. Time.*

Then I spot Natalie sashaying along the sidewalk, ear buds firmly planted. Eyes half closed like she's off in some musical dreamland, looking a bit buzzed. The Pink Girls spot her at the exact same moment as me and they all freeze.

Natalie doesn't even notice them all staring at her, whispering and laughing. One is holding a can of soda pop. Suddenly she sends it sailing through the air, aiming straight for Natalie. Just as it's about to smash into her head, I give her a good hard shove. A moment later she's sprawled at my feet. The pop can has crash-landed nearby and is gushing brown liquid.

"What the *hell*!" she yelps.

"What? Didn't you see the pop can?"

When I reach a hand out to help her, she slaps it away and pulls herself to her feet. Clearly, she didn't see it. "No mercy. None of you. You're all the same." And she stalks away.

The Pink Girls are killing themselves laughing now. And I'm totally mortified that Natalie would even equate me with those idiots. I completely ignore them, turn around and head for home.

3

CUT ME LOOSE

"Estelle!" Mom's voice jolts me out of a dinnertime daydream, yet another one of my band fantasies. She's standing by the counter, about to scoop some canned chili into a bowl from the pot on the stove, so she can go back and eat it in front of the TV. We're having it with soda crackers. It's slimy, almost impossible to swallow.

"What?"

"I asked you a question. Do we have any more crackers anywhere? You two finished this whole frigging sleeve."

"Somewhere on the counter, Mom," I tell

her, waving in the direction of the piled up
cartons and boxes. She and Stan are both staring at me. Stan has a stupid grin on his face.
"What are *you* looking at?"

"What are *you* so spazzed out about?" He
slurps up a spoonful of the gross mush. "It's
like you're in a trance or something, freak-
azoid."

"Suck my socks, Stan," I tell him. "You are
such a huge a-hole." I give him the finger with
both hands. Stan grins again and burps an in-
distinct reply.

"Estelle," Mom murmurs in her strange
half-voice. "Lose the attitude."

I roll my eyes and throw my spoon at Stan.
It sails past his head across the kitchen where
it clatters against the wall, leaving a big brown
splatter of chili before it hits the floor. Knowing that, *yet again*, as Stan likes to say, I'm
doomed. Wait for it —

"That's it! You're grounded again tonight,
Estelle," Mom calls out, and Stan's laughter
chases me down the hall.

At 10:30, after checking that Mom is snoring in her chair, I make my getaway out my window. I slip along in the shadows, heading for the place where everyone usually meets, an iron staircase leading down to the ravine. It's almost *too* easy.

I wish I could find somebody with a flask of Captain Morgan, or burning a joint or something, but clearly there's not much going on tonight. The dead-end street leading to the staircase is practically deserted, only one car parked close up to the bushes. Probably somebody making out, I'm thinking as I edge up for a closer look. I hear laughter and the clink of bottles spilling out the open window into the night. There's a whiff of cigarette smoke in the air.

The car looks familiar. I creep closer, try to get a better look. That can't be my dad's PT Cruiser parked there. Then I spot the vanity plate. REVMEUP. Yep, Dad's car.

My brother has this distinctive cackle that's contagious sometimes. And those giddy giggles are definitely coming from a girl. Gross.

How weird. Since when is Stan so chummy with Dad that he's allowed to borrow the car? Confused, I whip around in the other direction without even noticing what's coming until I'm flat on my butt on the sidewalk.

"Are you okay?"

I look up and all I can see is a black silhouette against the orange glow of a distant streetlight. Then a gloved hand reaches out to help me up and I realize it's Natalie. "Oh, it's *you*," she says in a dismissive voice. "Well, *are* you? Okay?"

"Yeah, I'm good," I tell her, standing up and brushing off the butt of my jeans, tugging on my tank top. "Thanks for asking."

She turns to walk away without giving me a chance to say anything else. But I do it anyway, because I know I have to.

"Wait," is what I call out to her.

She stops and turns around. I can't believe the difference in the two of us.

Her face is as white as sun-bleached bones. Under the streetlight, there's a glint of metal studs and hoops in her ears. Her black hair gleams. Her eyes seem bruised with eyeliner and mascara, her lips are a black stain. Her black skirt nearly reaches the tops of her Doc Martens. Stark white hands with black nails protrude from a filmy black shirt with a gaping rip held together with pins.

"Look, I'm really sorry about what happened this afternoon. You didn't give me a chance to explain things over at the plaza." When I take a step towards her, she takes one back and holds up a hand.

"I was trying to *stop* you from getting smashed in the head," I babble out. "I pushed you to *help* you. I wasn't even *with* the Pink Girls!"

Natalie smirks a little then. "Whatever, okay, apology accepted. I'm used to being bugged by them anyway. So is someone chasing you or what?" She has such a smoky, distinctive voice, even when she's just talking.

"Nope?" My answer comes out like a question.

"So why were you running?"

"Something I saw."

"Like what?" Natalie looks half-curious now.

"Like nothing. It's not important."

"Right." She examines her fingernails for a second. "So I hear you're starting a band."

"Says who?"

Natalie shrugs. "I'm Karim's Facebook friend. And you need a lead singer. He posted something about it in his status like half an hour ago."

I shake my head. "Karim updates way too much."

"Yeah, so true. Got any butts?" She raises her eyebrows hopefully.

"Nope. Sorry."

"Okay, well, I'm outta here." Natalie spins around and walks away.

Just now she sounded like every other girl

our age. Maybe she really would be a good fit for our band. Maybe she makes me nervous because of her dark funkiness. Guess it's just not my style. I should say something to her about coming to Lu's on Saturday. Before I can even open my mouth, she's melted away into the dark. So I head for home myself even though it's the last place I want to be.

I make a getaway again late Sunday morning before Stan even gets up. I don't even feel like looking at his face today.

Lying on Lu's bed in her groovy room, I stare up at the ceiling where a huge multi-coloured dragon kite is suspended from invisible wires. It looks as if it's broken loose from its string and is flying away. She strums her guitar, trying to put words to music, while we brainstorm new lyrics.

"*Cut me loose.*" The phrase pops into my head.

"What? Cut me loose?" Lu tilts her head at me.

"That would be a good song title, don't you think? How about this? *Cut me loose. Let me go. Why you're hanging on I'll never know.*"

"Yeah. Keep going." Lu tosses a notepad and pen at me. I start to scribble as she messes with some chords. "You seem to have some good angst going right now. Usually the best time to write a song."

"So how come you're always coming up with awesome lyrics when you have such a perfect life, Lulu?" I can't help but ask her.

Lu's eyes shift and she smirks at me over her guitar.

"Yeah, *real* perfect." She snickers. "Nobody does, Stelle, trust me."

"Come on, your parents are cool! I've seen them lots of times. Actually sitting together having a glass of wine and watching a movie in your family room!"

Lu frowns and rolls her eyes at me.

Words are filling my head now, pouring out through my pen as my angst swells.

Cut me loose. Let me go.
Why you're hanging on I'll never know.
Sever the string, break the tie,
let me loose, let me fly.
Set me free. Leave me alone.
I'd be so much better on my own.
It's time to cut me loose and let me go,
I really think that you should know . . .

As I scribble down the words, I know that Lu is watching me.

"Something's bugging you big time," she whispers. "It's more than just your mom not 'getting' you."

I just shrug and shake my head. I'm not ready to share the rest of it, how bad it's getting now with my mom. How buried I'm beginning to feel in my house.

It's way easier to ignore if my best friend doesn't know that the problems exist.

4

MERRY-GO-ROUND

All day at school on Monday, I find it hard to concentrate. Even after school, walking to the bus stop with Karim, I'm still half in a daze.

"Birthday," Karim whispers beside my ear, and I flash a quick grin at him before tuning out again. "Are you okay, Stelle?" His face is right up close to my head like he's trying to peer into my brain through my ear.

"I'm okay, Karim," I say, and don't offer another word.

"So it's Nana Day, isn't it? Maybe that's your problem today."

Knowing me so well, he's aware of my

weekly commitment to Nana. I do it every Monday to get it over with, so I won't have to worry about it for the rest of the week. Mom used to go now and then, but hasn't been in months. And Stan would never go. He can't face it.

Mom's brother and sister live across the country, so they never see Nana. It's left up to me. And I really don't mind so much. Nana was a great lady before she totally lost it. She was like my best friend, and now I don't think she even knows who I am.

I go anyway, though. To the nursing home where they keep her now. A lot of first-time visitors think she's a volunteer, tidy and trim in her jeans and sweaters, her long grey hair in a neat ponytail. That's how she managed to escape a couple of times from her high security wing. If only they'd notice that she's always wearing *slippers*. She usually comes back with candy that she's stolen from a nearby convenience store.

The bus drops me right in front of The

Golden Age Nursing Home. And as usual, I draw a deep breath before heading towards the entrance. It's a sprawling complex, all on one floor. There's a chronic care wing, a couples' wing, for those lucky enough to have grown old together, and a singles' wing. And then Nana's wing, where all the muddled people dwell.

"Hi, Stelle," Mrs. Moony says to me when I reach the greeter's desk. "How are you today?"

"Okay, I guess." I try to muster up a smile as I head for Nana's room.

I guess I should at least *try* to look happy in this place, there are so many sad faces everywhere. Sometimes it's hard to even distinguish the men from the women. They all seem to have the same blunt haircuts and ugly track suits, the same blank eyes. In the background, constantly playing like the soundtrack from hell, tinny music wafts from wall speakers.

I punch in the numbers on the keypad and the locked door clicks open. Then I hurry through the lobby, taking quick peeks into the lounge where poor sad people are sitting staring at a TV screen. Then I spot Nana down the hallway, slipping out of someone else's room with something tucked under her arm.

"Nana," I call out as I approach her. "What are you doing?" She has a bad habit of sneaking into the rooms of some of the residents and pilfering their stuff. Right now she's making off with a stuffed toy cat.

When I reach her, I peck her on her strangely smooth cheek. She's seventy-five years old, yet her cheek is still almost as smooth as peach skin.

"You're late," Nana snaps back at me.

"Late? I always get here around four o'clock on Mondays, Nana."

"And stop calling me Nana, Donna. Why do you call me Nana?"

Donna. That's my mom's name. Nana didn't call me anything but 'dear' after her family placed her here a couple of years back when she was diagnosed with Alzheimer's and couldn't live alone any more. Then she started calling me Donna a few months ago. I keep trying to jog her memory by reminding her who I really am.

"It's *Estelle*," I tell her gently as I lead her towards her room. "Donna is your daughter. I'm your *grand*daughter."

Nana hands me the stuffed cat. "Here. I bought you something."

"Thanks, Nana." I hand it off to an understanding nurse passing in the hallway, to return it to its rightful owner.

Nana's room is stark and sterile. There's a bed, an empty dresser, a chair, and that's it. She keeps all her clothes packed in a suitcase in her closet as if she'll be leaving on a trip soon. Nana sits on her bed and stares at me. There's an odd look in her eye. And she's cocking her head as though she's trying to unscramble something.

"Donna," she says, and I brace myself. "Why do you do such terrible things all the time?"

"What? What do you mean . . . M-Mom?" Might as well humour her.

"You know exactly what I mean, Donna. Running around with those lowlife friends of yours. Always missing your curfew, sneaking out of the house at night. I *know* what you're up to, Donna. Why do you try to hurt me so much?"

"Huh?" Is she talking about me or my mom?

"It's ever since you started with that crazy music business. You're just not the same any-more."

"Crazy music business?" Now I'm totally perplexed.

"You know what I mean. Quit playing the little innocent, Donna. You're going to get yourself in big trouble some day."

What is she babbling about? That's when I remind myself how little I know about my own mother's past. She's never shared any-thing. All I know is she finished high school, then took some kind of library technician course at college. Then married my dad, her high-school sweetheart. The rest is just a great big blank.

Now I'm curious, but it's too late. Nana is someplace else. She's gone over to the window where she's pulled the curtain aside to stare out at something.

"When did they put up that merry-go-round, Miss?" She has such a look of childish joy on her face that I have to check and see if there really is one. But no, it's just a congested parking lot and a busy street outside the window.

I almost feel like weeping when I leave. I miss the old Nana, the one who used to invite me for sleepovers, who taught me how to knit and how to bake pies. How can she stand living in this waiting room for the graveyard? And why can't they find a way to make it happier here for all these lonely, desolate people?

Maybe it's better that Nana doesn't even know where she is. And that she sees merry-go-rounds outside her window.

5

BABY BUMPS

The next morning at my locker, I keep one eye on the Pink Girls. They're tangled up in such a tight knot of spandex and denim that it's hard to tell where one girl ends and the other one begins. Sort of like a snake pit, I can't help thinking.

"Birthday soon." I spin around. Karim is standing there.

"*Really*?" I say, laughing. "Whose?" He waggles his thick eyebrows at me, then glances at the knot of girls. "What a bunch of divas. I love the T-shirt on that one, though. Great colour."

"It looks like toxic bubblegum," I tell him.

"You don't know from colour," he says, grinning wickedly.

Karim is so totally into fashion. He loves fabric, fingers all the clothes in stores whenever we're at the mall.

He experiments with used clothing that he picks up at Goodwill and Value Village, transforms what looks like trash into this amazing vintage funk / punk wear. Sews everything by hand. And dreams of the real sewing machine he wants to buy with his birthday money this year so he can design 'stagewear' for us.

"God, they're all the same, aren't they," I tell him. "No diversity whatsoever."

"And the Natalie kind of diversity would be *way* cool for your band?"

"Why are you and Lu so freaking fixated on that girl?"

"Well, for one thing, she has an awesome fashion sense. You know those crazy fishnet things she wears on her arms? They're actually tights. She cuts the crotch out, cuts the feet off, pulls them over her head, slides her arms through the legs. And wears them like some kind of funky shirt *under* her torn T-shirts. How cool is that?"

All I can do is shrug. That's definitely not my kind of cool, anyway. It makes Karim happy to see kids breaking out of the mould, embracing their individuality. And a happy Karim is a good Karim.

"Birth. Day. To. Morrow," he whispers, and yet again I crack up.

—————

After school I head over to Dad's place to smash out my frustrations on the drums. Josie greets me at the door. Is it my imagination or is that baby bump even bigger now than it was just a few days ago?

"Hi, sweetie," she says, and air kisses my cheeks. "How was school today?"

"Okay, I guess. Not as good as I would have liked it to be, though."

"Oh, sweetie," she touches my arm, her eyes suddenly wide and sympathetic. "Is there anything you want to talk about?" Josie has fabricated this terrific 'family' relationship that doesn't even exist.

"No thanks, Josie. It's kind of personal. Don't worry, I'll be fine."

"Well if there's ever *anything* you need, hon, you know where to find me. Oh, and your dad just called. He'll be home in a few minutes. Feel free to drum away."

Half an hour later, I'm totally lost in the beat when he appears in the doorway of my drum room. He has a sappy grin on his face. I ignore him even when he waves at me to stop. Headphones plugged into my iPod, I just keep on drumming along with Fleet Foxes *Helplessness Blues*. He walks over and lifts the set off my head.

"*Dad*! What are you *doing*?"

"Not even a 'hello', baby?" I hate it when he calls me baby.

"I'm practicing here, Dad. I hate being

interrupted when I'm practicing."

"What's wrong, Stelle?" He can see it. He's known me for so long, how could he possibly miss it? "You've been so cold and aloof lately."

He reaches out and touches my shoulder with one of those familiar hands, square palms and long fingers, so much like mine. Hands that used to pick me up and toss me, giggling, into the air, and rub my back when I needed comforting.

"I'm sure you'll figure it out sooner or later if you really think about it."

"Look, I know you're having a hard time facing this whole baby thing. And your mom's situation is no help either. But I'm *trying*, I really am. Your attitude is totally stressing Josie out, and that's not good for her right now."

A huge knot of fury tightens up my throat so I'm nearly choking. "Oh, so life's just not cushy enough for Josie right now, is it? *Crap* Dad, have you been to *our* place lately? You know, where you *used* to live."

He throws up his hands, spins around, and

walks away. The 'little girl' part of me wants to run after him and wrap my arms around his waist the way I used to. And burst into tears. But the more grown up part of me wants to yell at him not to let the door hit his ass on the way out.

Without another drumbeat, without another word, I slip through the back door and head for home.

Lu and I have a eureka telephone moment at supper time, and come up with the perfect present for Karim. Which is why we wind up at Goodwill on Tuesday evening. But instead of the local one that Karim is constantly cleaning out, we take the bus across town to another thrift shop. We hope to find bag-loads of used, and with luck even vintage, stuff for him to whip up into new creations. And it won't even cost much either!

We hit the mother lode, too. Find an assortment of tops and jeans that he can chop up and reinvent. Some paisley shirts from god knows when, and ribbed knitwear that he likes to turn into arm and leg warmers. A cool retro vest, and some funky old felt hats that smell a little of mothballs. All treasures for his creative hands and mind. We even toss in a well-used tambourine just for fun.

All the way home, each of us lugging a crammed tote bag, we babble about the cool stuff that Karim will be able to do with it all, and how hopefully, soon, he'll be designing for the band. Then I stop off at Lu's place to help her fold everything up and pack it into big sparkly shopping bags that we picked up at the dollar store.

After the bags are packed up and stuffed with glittery tissue paper, we sign a card for Karim. Tomorrow Lu will bring the presents over to my place at dinnertime, because Xing has promised to give her a drive. We can't wait 'til tomorrow to surprise Karim.

6

STITCHED UP

The bizarre thing is that Karim is missing in action on Wednesday. He hasn't shown up at school, which is odd for our friend. He never misses. And *if* he does, he always lets us know why. Lu finally tells me mid-morning that he texted her, *Meet you later at Stelle's dad's place.*

I head straight for my dad's place right after the last bell. Lu, and apparently Karim, will be showing up around 4:30. As soon as Josie opens the door, a delicious smell greets me. Baking chocolate. Is there anything better?

Josie gives me her usual air kisses then snags me by the arm and leads me into the kitchen. A scrumptious-looking chocolate cake decorated in pink and yellow sugar flowers is sitting on some sort of crystal pedestal.

"Voila," she says with a swoop of her arm. "Chocolate cake. You'll never guess what else it's made with. Black *beans*: a whole can," she tells me.

I almost gag. "Seriously?" I try to smile. "How totally . . . um, creative. Hmm, can't wait to taste it, I think."

Before I need to dream up something to talk about with Josie, the doorbell chimes and I rush to answer it. Lu's standing there with the two sparkly bags in one hand and her guitar in the other. When she steps into the foyer and looks around, her mouth-wide-open expression is a scream.

"Shoes off, babe," I tell her. "Rules, you know."

"How come you never told me your dad's living with Martha Stewart," she whispers with a straight face. I have to cover my mouth so Josie won't hear me laugh.

Josie gushes over Lu. Even gives *her* air kisses, says how thrilled she is that I'm finally bringing my friends over. A few seconds later, the doorbell rings again.

"The birthday boy!" I skate across the gleaming hardwood to answer.

I fling open the door. Karim is not smiling. He smells faintly of weed. His eyes are red, his black hair a dishevelled mess. So are his clothes, as if he just rolled out of bed. Then he crumples into my arms.

"What the hell happened to you?" I hear Lu saying behind me.

Karim pulls away. He digs into the pocket of his skinny vintage jeans, pulls out a crumpled piece of paper and hands it to us. Lu grabs it and reads out loud.

Stitched Up
Stitching my life together,
Bits and pieces of a brand new me,

But Frankenstein's monster,
Is what my people see

Some sordid creation,
Some nightmare stalker.
Doesn't matter if I walk or
Run away from who I am,
I always follow me,
Try to prove that I'm just like the rest,
Being the most I can be,
Just doing my very best.

Slicing through the fabric of my life
Splicing missing pieces,
A puzzle seeking sense,
A work-in-progress
Always sitting on the fence,
Be a man, they tell me,
Why don't you be a man.

Let's be honest,
I'm doing the best I can . . .

When Lu finishes reading, we all stand there in silence. Karim is staring at his retro red basketball sneakers. I actually see a couple of tears splash onto the shiny floor. Josie hovers in the background, looking distraught.

"What happened?" I whisper, and he slowly shakes his head.

"No birthday money this year," he says in a hoarse voice. "So I can't buy my sewing machine. Got a toolbox, fully loaded, instead." Then one side of his lip curls into the ghost of a smile. "If it wasn't so pathetic, it would almost be hilarious."

"God, that sucks," Lu murmurs.

"It sucks tons," Karim says. "My family with their culture-this and tradition-that all the time — they don't want to get me at all. And they will never ever be able to deal with . . . you know . . . *it*. Me. I would be like a black mark on the family name. I swear, they're going to disown me."

I never imagined it could be that bad for my friend. And here I thought my own family was a crazy mess. When I look over at Lu, her eyes are filling, just like mine, and I can practically read her thoughts. We both swoop Karim into a group hug. Over his shoulder I can see Josie, standing there stroking her stomach in a motherly way. And looking as if she's doing her best to resist rushing over to join our huddle.

He snuffles out a sob into my shoulder, then half laughs in his Karim way. "I'll be locked in the closet forever, the way my life is going right now. And there won't even be any cool new outfits in it either. Not without that sewing machine."

Josie touches his shoulder and smiles. "Okay," she says. "Who needs a slice of chocolate cake . . . *before* dinner!"

A few seconds later she's handed out forks and we all stand around the counter and dig into the Black Bean Chocolate Brownie Cake without even using plates.

"Chocolate fixes almost everything," Josie murmurs through a mouthful. "Guess what else, Karim. I have an electronic sewing machine. You can come over here and use it whenever you want."

Karim's eyes light up. "Seriously?" he says with new hope in his dark eyes.

"Of course. I'd never say it if I didn't mean it," Josie says, patting his hand.

Karim is smiling now. He's looking all around, checking the place out, shaking his head, stuffing his face.

"Can I live here?" he says. "I mean honestly, can I, Josie? I am dead serious."

With a serene smile Josie rubs her belly in slow circles.

"Remind me again," Lu says later that evening, "why it is you don't like Josie, Stelle? I mean sure, she sort of stole your dad, and he totally ditched your mom. But he's so happy with her, and with the baby coming . . ."

"Yeah, what's up with that anyway?" Karim says as he reaches for another handful of all-natural fruit jellies that Josie delivered in a crystal candy dish. "*Voila. Les bonbons*! She busts her butt to make you happy, and you don't even appreciate it!"

We've polished off the gigantic veggie pizza she made for us. Now we're down in my soundproof music room, jamming. We've already put Karim's lyrics to music, come up with a good bridge for it, and let him try singing. Dad is home now, having dinner with Josie. But she keeps coming down and checking on us. And putting a hand on Karim's shoulder, making sure he feels better.

"Interesting question, you guys," I tell them.

I realize I don't even have a solid answer for them. Probably because I'm not so sure myself anymore.

7

DRUM ROLL, PLEASE

On Saturday afternoon, I'm setting up my drum kit for practice in Lu's garage after getting dropped off by my dad. Karim bursts through the door wearing his Saturday Goodwill special. And he's carrying a box.

"Ta *da!*" he says, setting it down. Then he starts pulling stuff out. The tambourine we gave him, plus a set of cymbals, maracas, and a triangle. "Found all this other stuff at thrift shops! I am now officially in the band — the auxiliary percussionist!"

"Sweet! Major multitasker!" I tell him. "Manager and 'stagewear' designer, too."

Lu starts clapping and grinning. "That's brilliant, Karim. Just what we need!"

"And check this out!" He spins around, showing off his new duds. Thankfully he's recovered from his birthday letdown. Josie might have helped with that, I have to admit. "Got all this for under ten bucks! The jeans are vintage, I swear. *And* this Black Sabbath T-shirt from the seventies!"

"Ah, the funky punk and hard rock seventies," I sigh. "The decade before the glam metal and New Wave 80s when my mom was in high school. *Ewwy* music."

Lu looks up suddenly from tuning her guitar. Her eyes grow wide. "Yipes! I totally forgot to tell you what my mom told me. So yesterday she was visiting a friend and started telling her how we're starting up a band. And guess what? Her *friend* went to school with your *mom*, Stelle!"

"Really? Small world," I tell her with a shrug. "I know absolutely zip about what went on in my mom's high school years."

"And guess what *else* she told my mom." Lu's eyes are even wider now. "Your *mom* used to party hard in high school!"

"Say *what*?" Karim says. "*Donna Draper*?"

"Par*don*?" I say to her.

She tilts her head and grins wide. "Apparently your mom was some sort of alt rock-digging chick back in the 80s. Loved this band called the Bangles."

"*My* mom?" I'm practically choking on my incredulity. "Are you sure she got the right person?"

"*Your* mom, Stelle. My mom's friend pulled out her old yearbooks and showed her the photos. My mom recognized her name. Donna Draper, right?" I nod slowly, dumbfounded. "And . . ." Lu adds, "drum roll please. *Your* mom had a *band* too."

"No way. You lie." That's all I can think of saying.

"It's the truth. My mom's friend told her all about it. They called themselves '*Virago Girls*'. *And* they even wrote their own music."

"*Virago Girls*? I don't even know what that word *means*," I tell them.

"Come on. What kind of a 'grrrl' are you anyway?" Karim says. "A virago is a strong, domineering woman. A chick you don't want to mess with."

"That really is a cool name," Lu says. "Wow, Stelle, how come you never told us about all this, anyway?"

I sit down now on an overturned recycling bin because my knees have sort of buckled under me. "How am I supposed to tell you something that I don't even know about *my-self*? My mom is the total *opposite* of a virago."

"Haven't you ever looked at your mom's old school yearbooks? My mom's are hilarious," Lu tells us. "I check them out all the time. God, the styles! Those ridiculous sideways pony-tails. And the mullets and mohawks on some of the dudes were totally embarrassing."

Karim is clucking his disapproval and rolling his eyes. "The Eighties were a total fashion misfortune. I mean, those shoulder pads! And the tights and leg warmers. And painted-on jeans. *Gag me with a spoon*."

"I never even thought of asking to see their yearbooks," I confess. "I basically know squat about my parents' previous lives."

"What about your grandma? Mine always blabs about the trouble my mom got into as a teen. Didn't yours ever share with you?" Lu asks. "Oh, right. Your poor Nana . . ."

My poor befuddled Nana. She's been drifting away from me for so long now. But before she lost it, she only really told stories about my mom as a little kid. She never got into the teen years. Maybe there was a good reason for that.

She and Mom never seemed close, either. Mom never went out of her way to visit Nana very often, even before she turned into a recluse. About once a month she dropped me and Stan off for a Nana sleepover. She would come in for a cup of tea, but they never talked much. Just sat across from each other in this awkward silence.

And what about those strange questions Nana was asking me on Monday? About missing my curfew, and my lowlife friends, and that '*crazy music business*'. What went on between those two way back when, anyway? My mom was one of the *Virago Girls*?

Lu and Karim are just standing there and staring at me. They have a pretty good clue that things are pretty crappy at my house right now. But best friends should understand the whole messy story, right?

So I finally start pouring it all out, telling them how bad it's gotten since they last stepped through my door ages ago, before my dad split. How the layers and layers of junk have built up. How Mom freaks if we threaten to get rid of anything. How there's only a shell left of the person she once used to be. How it's all driving me way too crazy. We also talk about compulsive hoarding, since it seems to be all over the TV right now.

They envelop me in a huge hug. It feels good, almost like they're protecting me. Then Lu pulls away.

"Okay, so all that awful crap with your mom is totally fixable, right? There's shrinks and medication and clutter busters and all sorts of stuff. But hell, Stelle," Lu says, shaking her head. "Donna *a rocker*? Now *that* is totally twisted!"

"Babe," Karim adds, looking serious, "you've gotta find a way to help the old Donna Draper get her mojo back."

8

OVER AND OUT

The first thing I do when I get home is Google the word 'virago'. And of course, Wikipedia comes up with a nice concise definition: *a strong, brave, or warlike woman.*

I like that. I like the sound of it. I just can't fathom the fact that it could ever possibly be associated with my MOM! Next, I Google the words 'compulsive hoarder', and get a complete education on the subject. It's the first time I've considered the possibility that it's actually a clinical disorder my mom has. Basically, a mental problem. That sounds way more like a definition of my mom than 'virago' does. If she really does have a serious problem, how am I going to be able to help her sort it out when I can't even get her to take a shower?

She's ordered pizza for dinner on Saturday evening. Stan has even shown up for a change, but it looks like he's pumped to go out someplace. He doesn't waste any time scarfing back about six slices, and then bouncing without even saying goodbye. Then Mom and I are alone.

I don't even know how to talk to her anymore. But today I have to find a way.

"So, Mom?" It's hard to grab her attention. She's eating her third slice of pizza, licking sauce off her fingertips and staring at the TV screen. Some old sitcom is droning on. Not sure why she watches those, because I haven't heard her laugh in ages.

"Hmmm?" She swivels her head and looks at me with those sad, glassy eyes.

And a starting point leaps onto my lips.

"So I went to visit Nana on Monday."

"Did you?" she says in her slow voice.

"She was kind of muddled. Actually, for a while she thought I was *you*. She even called me Donna at one point."

"Guess she's really getting confused, huh?"

"Quite. And she said a few strange things to me, too, Mom."

"Strange how, Stelle?"

"Like she wondered why I sneak out of the house at night. And miss my curfew. And why I do such mean things all the time."

Slowly, my mom turns to face me again. Her eyes shift from side to side as if she's not quite willing to meet my gaze.

"And what did you tell her?"

"Well, nothing really because then she got all distracted again."

"Good." She looks away.

Good? "But she thought I was *you*, Mom."

"You just said she was muddled. You just proved your point."

"But before that she said something about my 'lowlife friends' and my 'crazy music business'. I just wondered what she meant by that."

"I have no idea," the back of her head tells me. "Muddled, remember?"

"How come you never go and visit her, Mom?"

"Oh, you know, I'm just too tired all the time."

"You can come with me on Mondays when I go," I offer. "I'll bet she'd be happy to see you there."

"We'll see. Oh, good. *Wheel of Fortune* is coming on next."

Over and out.

I've never liked the crawlspace. It's dim and musty, and the unfinished ceiling is too low. Plus it absolutely kills my back, crouching under there. But this time I've come prepared with a stool to sit on, and a flashlight to illuminate the gloom. Everything feels soggy under here and makes me think of rotting things. I'm terrified that I'm going to step on a mummified mouse carcass.

I should have worn gloves. Hesitantly I start lifting cardboard flaps and peering inside, only to discover yet another box of smelly clothes or college textbooks, or old dolls and stuffed toys that mom played with as a *little girl*. There are even Christmas and Halloween decorations we haven't put up for years. Nothing worth salvaging.

But wait. This looks intriguing. One of the flaps I've just lifted reveals the narrow spines and hard covers of something that appears to be . . . yes! Yearbooks. And there's something else in the box, too, preserved in some sort of a plastic envelope. Through the plastic I can read the words '*virago songbook*'. I suck in my breath. Jackpot!

I gather up as much as I can carry and stumble up the basement steps to my room. Then in the hallway I trip over a stack of newspapers and drop the entire load.

"Stelle! What are you *doing*?" Mom's voice startles me. Why isn't she asleep on the sofa yet?

"Nothing, Mom!" I retrieve my treasures and dart into my bedroom before she can notice what I'm carrying.

9

ROCK CHICK

It's true, what Lu's mom told her. My mom really was an alt rock chick.

There's four years worth of yearbooks and as I flip through them, it's like a revelation. Mom and Dad, Donna Draper and Wally Czulinski, from Grades 9 through 13, looking a bit older every year. The two of them transforming from gawky 'niners', spotty with zits, into self-assured grads. Hairstyles morphing before my eyes, Mom's getting longer and more poofed up each year. And Dad, with a long mullet that makes me embarrassed *for* him. My mom and dad in the drama club, photos of a rehearsal for *The Music Man*. My parents in the *drama* club?

It's a pop culture archive. Even the scrawled autographs at the back of the book reveal a little about my parents and their 'era'. *"Stick 2gether you 2"* and *"U ROCK, Virago Girl!"* and *"Killer songs, Donna"* and *"Never forget Saturday hotboxin' at Bobby's"*. What? And yes, there are a couple of grainy photos of a band on stage at some sort of Battle of the Bands, with the caption *'Virago Girls Rocking Out'*. My mom is holding the mic. She's dressed in some sort of short, tight black shift. And yes, my mom is actually on stage singing and she looks *really* good!

I am in total shock. And I still haven't even opened the 'virago songbook' yet.

But I don't get a chance. Because there's a tapping noise at my window that scares the crap out of me. When I peek out, Lu and Karim's faces are pressed against the glass grinning madly at me. Karim has a tightly rolled joint between his teeth.

"Come on," Lu says when I open the sash. "Let's go chill at the iron stairway."

I need to get out for a while. I can still taste the mustiness from the crawlspace. I pop out the screen, scramble over the windowsill and drop to the dirt.

Our butts planted on the cold metal, we sit at the very top of the steps. Gaze out across the moonlit park, enjoying the comfortable silence as only good friends can. It's all silver and shadows below us, swathed in light from a moon that's nearly full or nearly not. A wisp of wind stirs the treetops. Karim sparks the joint, and passes it around. And after a few tokes, he starts totally mellowing out.

"The moonlight is cool, isn't it? Like everything's dipped in silver or something," Karim whispers after a while. "And look at all the stars up there. I mean, do you ever wonder what it's all about? Like, are we the only ones in this entire friggin' universe?"

"Don't go getting all philosophical on us, dude," I tell him. "You always do it when you're buzzed."

And then, behind us, on the dead end road that ends at the iron steps, there's the sound of tires crunching on gravel. We all turn our heads in the direction of the sound. We can hear music blaring and an engine purring then shutting off. But the music is still on, and I have a feeling I know who's parked there.

"Let's go check out who's partying in that car." Karim stands up and starts edging back along the pathway to the parking area.

"Ha, nice wheels. A PT Cruiser? Who drives a Cruiser around here?" Lu says. "Wait, doesn't your dad drive one, Stelle?"

I hear a girl giggling and shrieking a bit. Then my brother laughing hysterically.

Lu cocks her head. "Hey, I know that laugh. Isn't that your —"

I push past Karim and Lu on the pathway

because I can't *wait* to see Stan's face when I knock on the windshield and peer inside.

Knock, knock, knuckles on glass. "Hey, bro. How's it goin'?"

"Wow," Karim says over my shoulder.

"Nice rack," Lu says.

"Holy crap! *Stelle*?" My brother looks like he's about to barf. "What the hell are *you* doing here?"

I'm totally revelling in the look of shock on his face. And on Camilla's, from our school. Her shirt is off, and I can see her skimpy little pink lace bra as she scrambles to tug her shirt on over her head. She shakes her cascade of thick blonde hair and sits there trying to look cool while she lights up a smoke.

"Holy crap, *Stan*. What the hell are *you* doing driving Dad's car?"

Then, without even skipping a beat, he breaks it to me.

"Dad and I have an arrangement, Stelle. You know, like *you* do with the drums. No blabbing to Mom, okay?"

"Wow, looks like we're even then, huh?" I shake my head and walk away.

Hunched over my keyboard trying to write an English essay on *Othello* Sunday afternoon, I'm totally distracted by The Bangles.

I keep checking out their old performances on YouTube. And reading their lyrics. I like their stuff. It reminds me of what Lu and I have been trying to write, especially "I'll Set You Free", and "Manic Monday". I can't believe how much I identify with these lyrics. I've e-mailed the link to Lu, and she agrees with me, so we might try to cover some Bangles songs at some point.

And the entire time I'm sort-of-working on my essay, something is niggling at my brain. Something I was about to do, something that seemed really important at the time. Wait! The Virago songbook! I start flinging aside the yearbooks that I left scattered on my carpet last night. And there it is. Clipped inside an old black duo-tang folder with missing teeth, the cover worn so soft from use that it almost feels like suede. Careful not to tear any of the pages, I begin flipping through it slowly.

These song lyrics have been thwacked out on an old-fashioned typewriter. I can even see the globs of white-out where she made mistakes. The titles are attention grabbers. *I Own My Own Heart; Circle of Psychosis; Aching to be Free; Catastrophe in Black; Back 2 Back 2 Basics; Stuck Inside of Me; Alone Afraid.* I'm starting to get impressed. These are really cool titles. And the lyrics are poetic and passionate.

Wow, my mom might have actually been cool, once upon a time. But what happened? I tuck the songbook into my backpack for safe-keeping and flop onto my bed to think for a while, but my eyes don't stay open for long.

It's late afternoon when I wander out of my room to find something to eat. Stan's leaning against the kitchen counter, chewing on a piece of cold pizza and staring into space. He looks as if he's still recovering from a bad night.

"So how's Camilla, Stan?" I ask him, just to bug him. "You seeing her again tonight? Going parking in Dad's car?"

"Camilla? Oh, is that her name? Not sure I'm *ever* seeing her again."

"What a complete jackass you are. You know that?"

"Whatever. Her body totally rocks, though!" He starts howling laughing and I grab a cup from the sink and pitch it at his head. Luckily it's made of plastic and bounces right off his thick skull. Then I throw some random cutlery that's been drying on the rack. It all goes clattering onto the kitchen floor when Stan ducks. Then Mom starts hollering from the living room.

"You're making me crazy! What the hell are you two doing out there?"

"Nothing," Stan yells back, then throws a piece of pizza at me. I snatch it midair as it's flying past.

"Thanks. I was looking for something to eat."

I take a bite out of it then walk away.

A TOTAL MESS

I'm madly playing catch-up in study hall on Monday, when there's a rustling sound beside me. I look up to see Natalie standing there.

"Hey, how's it going?" she murmurs.

"Okay," I whisper back, my eyes shifting between my paper and the study hall supervisor who's already eyeballing us. "What's up?"

"Not much," she says. "So anyway . . ." She pauses. "Did you find a lead singer for your band yet? Word's out that you're getting desperate."

Karim on social media yet again, no doubt. "Still working on it," I tell her.

"Well, I'm available," she says. "Just thought I should mention it."

"Thanks. I'll keep that in mind, Nat."

"You guys write your own lyrics, don't you?"

"Yup, we do."

"I'd love to read them. How long have you been playing drums?"

"A few years now." My drums! I miss them! I left them at Lu's on Saturday and I haven't touched them since.

"And how long has Lu been on the guitar?"

"'Bout the same, I guess."

"I play the guitar, too. And write songs. We should get together. Sometime. If you guys feel like it."

I pause. She sounds hesitant, almost nervous.

"Sure, that might work," I tell her. Better not blow this chance or I'm doomed! Better invite her to drop over on Saturday.

"Well, see ya, Stelle." Natalie, in her billowy layers, is drifting off out of study hall. I can't call out to invite her or the supervising teacher will freak. So I scoop up all my school stuff, then run after her.

"Hey, Natalie, hang on a sec," I call, then I hurry up behind her.

But before I can even reach her, someone pushes past me in a pink and denim blur, and dumps a super-size Mr. Sub cupful of cola and ice cubes right over Natalie's head. She gasps and shrieks and shakes her arms off, as a knot of girls goes racing away down the hall and around the corner. Then her eyes narrow and she glares at me.

"How come you're standing right there every time something crappy happens to me?" she says, wiping cola off her face with her sleeve.

She spins around and stalks off down the hall towards the washroom, leaving a puddle of cola and ice cubes behind. Along with a stunned bunch of babbling, texting kids who just watched the whole thing happen and can't shut up about it. And my chance is gone again. And Natalie is mad at me again.

I know today isn't going to improve any either. After all, it's Nana Day.

———

As soon as I enter Nana's room, I know something is wrong. There's a strong odour of urine. Usually Nana is up and dressed, wandering from room to room. But today she's in bed, wearing a nightgown and looking sallow and weak. She's just staring into space.

"Nana? Are you okay?"

She raises her head to look at me, and sits there blinking like a baby bird.

"That's it." I march out into the hallway and straight over to the nursing station. "Has anyone noticed that my grandmother is sitting in a puddle of her own urine?" I ask a startled nurse.

"I'm sorry, who are we talking about?"

"I'm talking about my Nana in that room right *there*," I say, jabbing my finger in the direction of her door. "Why isn't anyone looking after her?"

"Oh, of course. We're really understaffed here, dear. Have your Nana press her buzzer and someone will be right there."

"I'm not even sure she knows where the button *is*. I'm not sure she even knows where *she* is. She sees a merry-go-round outside her window! Just send someone to her room *right away*, okay?"

"I'll do my best," she tells me without even looking up from her computer.

I march back to the room and press the buzzer hard at least five times. Then I go to the door and peer out into the hallway. All I see is an orderly pushing a meal cart.

"Okay, Stelle, you can do this yourself. You can't just leave her here like this." I head down the hall to snatch some clean linens and a hospital gown off a trolley.

Gingerly I lift back the covers on her legs so I can pull her nightgown off. The first thing I see is her feet, with their long, yellowed toenails, almost like chicken feet. Gross! Her legs are so skinny and scary-looking with age spots and dark blue veins. Thank goodness she's wearing underwear at least.

I concentrate on tugging the nightgown over her head. Gulp. No bra! Then, thankfully, I hear the squeak and swish of an approaching nurse, who breezes into the room looking concerned.

"What are you *doing*?" she says.

"What does it *look* like I'm doing?" I snark. "Nobody came when I was buzzing so I have to do it myself!"

"We're all tied up," she hastily explains. "Sorry someone couldn't get here sooner. I'll take it from here, sweetie."

Then suddenly her whole demeanour shifts. She tenderly strokes Nana's forehead and sticks an electronic thermometer into her ear. "You look like you're having some problems today, Mrs. Draper." The nurse turns to me. "She might have a bladder infection. I'll find out." Then she touches my arm. "Thanks for your help here."

"It's okay. Sorry I was so crabby with you.

I'm just worried about my Nana, that's all." And when tears jump into my eyes, the nurse squeezes my shoulder.

"You really are a lovely granddaughter for taking such good care of your Nana. Nobody else from your family ever visits, do they?"

"You think your nursing staff is stressed out?" I tell her. "You should meet my family. It's a *total* mess. We put the 'fun' in dysfunctional."

She smiles in sympathy, then gets to work on Nana and I head for home. It feels so good to push through the exit and out into the fresh air and daylight.

As soon as I step through the front door I know that something is wrong. Mom isn't on the sofa the way she always is when I get home from Nana's on Mondays. In fact, the house is eerily silent and my armpits prickle.

"Mom?" No answer. "MOM?" Still no answer.

When I peer down the hallway, I see my mother's legs and feet, wearing striped socks, sticking out from the bathroom into the hall. They look like the legs of the Wicked Witch of the East after the house fell on her. Even though I'm afraid to, I know I have to look. And when I do, I can't breathe for an instant. She's lying there in her nightgown, so white and still with her eyes half open, I'm pretty sure she might be dead. But no, her chest is moving.

So I call 9-1-1. Then I sit down beside her and listen for the sound of sirens.

11

PANIC ATTACK

She starts coming to in the ambulance. Then she just lies there, sort of blinking and staring at me and at the paramedics.

"What am I doing here?" she says in a muffled voice from behind the oxygen mask.

"They're not sure, Mom. They think you passed out for some reason. They're taking you to Emergency."

"No! I don't *want* to go there. Tell them to take me home."

"No, Mom. You hurt yourself when you fell. They have to check you over."

By then the EMTs have detected the huge

lump on her head. They figured it must have just happened. And they explain that they need to check her over to make sure there's no sign of concussion.

Then, after a few minutes of staring and looking completely muddled, Mom starts shaking. And I mean earthquake shaking. Then she starts crying, and I mean out-of-control sobbing. The paramedics exchange these looks. One of them mutters *panic attack* with a question in her voice.

It's a total relief when they wheel her away once we've reached the hospital ER. Then I have to sit and wait and wonder what the hell is going on with my mom.

It's actually a relief when Dad and Stan finally come blasting through the sliding ER doors, but, oh no, Josie is with them, too. Why did Dad have to bring *her* along? She plops her ample baby girth down right beside me.

"You okay, Stelle?" she says. Dad slips in on the other side of me, then squeezes my shoulder.

"I guess I'm sort of fine," I tell them as my eyes well up.

Stan sits across from me. His face looks almost greyish.

"How bad was it?" he says in a quiet voice.

"It was awful. I thought she was dead."

Stan gulps hard and looks down at his knees.

"Have you heard anything from the doctor yet?" Dad says. He lays his big sturdy hand on top of mine. It feels safe and good.

"Still waiting, Dad."

We all sit in silence, staring at the door. I feel numb and exhausted, and my ears have a faraway buzzing deep inside. I wish I could just go to bed and sleep until this is all over. Then the door swings open and a doctor steps into the room.

"Are you Mrs. Czulinski's family?"

"I guess that's what you could call us," Dad says, glancing around at all of us. "Donna is actually my *ex*-wife, though."

"That's fine. I'm Doctor Kako." He reaches out his hand and Dad shakes it.

"Wally Czulinski."

"And these are your children?"

Stan laughs out loud at that one, and Josie's face drops.

"Yes . . . I mean, no . . . I mean, yes and no!" Dad is clearly mortified.

Stan laughs even louder. Josie's face has turned crimson. She stands up and reaches out her hand. Flustered, Dr. Kako shakes it. "I'm Josie Kincaid," she explains glancing at my dad. "Stan and Stelle are Wally's children from his marriage to Donna Czulinski."

The doctor half nods, half-smiles and coughs quickly. "I see," he says. "Well, Donna had a pretty severe blow to her head so we'll have to keep her in for observation. She also has some symptoms of panic disorder. We've given her a mild sedative to help her rest."

Dr. Kako then turns to me. "And you are Stelle? Your mother asked to see you for a moment."

Surprised, I stand up. My legs feel as if

they're made of Silly Putty. The doctor places his hand on my shoulder.

"You found your mother on the bathroom floor today, didn't you?"

"That's right," I whisper.

"And can I assume that you're the one who spends the most time with her?"

When I look over at Stan, he slides down in his chair, hoodie pulled up over his head. "That's right, Doctor. It's mostly me and my mom."

"I'd like to talk to you about your mom for a couple of minutes if that's okay."

"Sure," I tell him, and he leads me out of the waiting room and into the hallway. When I spin a glance over my shoulder, my so-called family is staring at me with dread.

Dr. Kako asks me a whole slew of questions about my mom and her habits. I babble like crazy, telling him all the horrible details of her sad life. He's not much taller than me, and has sort of a calm disposition as he nods and scribbles, frowns and smiles. I feel so comfortable talking to him that I go right into the problem with Nana today. He looks concerned, and shakes his head.

"You haven't had a very good day, have you, Stelle?" he says. When I shake my head, unable to speak, he leads me to a counter and hands me a box of tissues. "Are you ready to see your mom now?"

I nod again, then follow him down the hallway to a big room with six beds, ceiling-to-floor curtains wrapped around each of them. When we step behind the curtain, she's lying there with her eyes closed, very pale. When she hears the curtain sliding closed again, she stirs and her eyes flutter open.

"Stelle?" she murmurs, struggling with her lids.

"Yeah, it's me, Mom," I tell her. She reaches her hand from beneath the sheets, gropes for mine. Her hand is cold. I can see grime under her fingernails. She squeezes and I squeeze back.

"You okay?" That's *her* asking *me*!

"I should be asking you that. How are you feeling, Mom?"

"Tired, Stelle. But really relaxed. Am I going home now?"

"I'm afraid not, Mrs. Czulinski," the doctor says. "You've had a bad fall. We have to keep an eye on you for a bit and run a few tests."

"I fell?" she says. "When did I fall?"

"She can't even *remember* that?" I ask Doctor Kako.

"Slight amnesia," he explains. "It'll all come back to her soon enough."

"Why am I so tired?" She's struggling to keep her eyes open.

"We've given you a very mild sedative to help you relax," he tells her.

"Feels good," she mutters. "Are you staying here with me, Stelle?"

"Should I?" I ask the doctor.

"I think your mom needs to rest now, and we'll be taking her for tests later tonight. You might as well go home with your family and give us a call in the morning. Then you can come back for another visit tomorrow. You understand Mrs. Czulinski?"

Mom nods. I'm relieved. I don't think I could handle sitting here holding her hand for hours. I kiss Mom's forehead and slip out through the curtains. When I get back to the waiting room, their faces haven't changed. It's as if they've stayed frozen with dread the whole time I've been gone.

I laugh out loud when I see them. It's the first time I've laughed all day.

12

REAL PERFECT

After the hospital, we all stop for dinner at Swiss Chalet. I scarf down a salad, a half chicken, and pile of fries while Dad and Stan debate the next move.

"I'm not so sure you two should stay home by yourselves," Dad keeps insisting. "It would be better for you to stay with Josie and me until this all gets settled."

"Come on, Dad. I'm nearly nineteen. Stelle's nearly sixteen. Obviously we can handle it on our own. We're not little kids anymore, remember?" Stan tells him.

After listening to them state their cases

for a few minutes, I finally bust into their discussion.

"Well, I don't care what you do, Stan. But I'm staying with Dad and Josie whether you do or not." I lick sauce off my fingertips and smile at them. "Maybe Josie will even cook for us."

Josie gives my arm a grateful squeeze. "Of course I will, Stelle. I'd love that."

Stan shakes his head. "God, okay, whatever. I guess I can give it a shot. But just 'til we find out what's going on with Mom."

Dad looks almost relieved. Then I come up with a suggestion of my own.

"I think we should try to get rid of some of the junk in the house while Mom is in the hospital. I mean, Stan and I try our best, keep the bathroom clean and wash the dishes. But all that excess *stuff* needs to be gone for good."

Everyone stares at me for an instant, as if I've just told them that I think the world is really flat. Then a light bulb goes on over Stan's head and he starts nodding.

"Yeah, Stelle. I like that idea. We could get some of those industrial strength garbage bags and unload all the crap she gathered."

"It wouldn't be so tough to just load up a bunch of those clear recycling bags with all the newspapers. And we could drop off some boxes of stuff at Goodwill."

"Has it gotten that *bad*?" Dad looks shocked.

"How long since you've stepped through the door, Dad?" I ask him.

"Long time, I guess. Couple of years since I left."

"You can't even believe it now," Stan says. "I swear the stuff is breeding."

"Really that bad, huh?" He shakes his head and sighs.

"Oh, Dad, you can't even begin to imagine," I tell him. "It could be some sort of clinical disorder that Mom has, you know."

"That would explain a lot of things," Stan says. "So, okay, why don't you drop us off after dinner, Dad? We can pick up some school clothes and stuff, then walk over to your place. Tomorrow after school, we can start shovelling out the dump we live in."

"Let's do it!" I high five my brother. "But I have to stop at the home to check on Nana first." Then I tell them all about the condition Nana was in when I went there today. Dad stares into his empty plate the entire time, while Stan pushes a chicken bone around with his fork. "You two remember her, don't you? How come nobody even bothers to ask about her anymore?"

"No need to get nasty, Stelle," Dad says in a sheepish voice.

"Is there anything I can do to help?" Josie asks me.

"Come on now, Josie. It's not really your problem, honey," Dad says, patting her hand. She pulls it away from him again.

"I think I can make up my own mind, Wally. Honest, Stelle, if you want me to go over there and look in on your Nana tomorrow, I won't mind at all."

"Really?" I'm stupefied. Why is Josie being so nice? Or maybe she really just *is* nice. Hmmm. "That would be amazing, Josie. If you have the time, I mean."

"Oh, I have plenty of time. I'm getting bored as hell around the house."

"You are?" Dad says. "But I thought you liked —"

"Bookkeeping? And cleaning, cooking, and doing your laundry for you? Oh yeah, it's just great. I miss being around people, Wally. I need to get out."

Dad's eyes are wide. His mouth is open. "Whatever you say, honey."

"Damn right," Josie says, then gives me a high five.

What the hell is going on around here today? I'm so relieved that I order a huge piece of Caramel Chocolate Cheesecake Explosion just to celebrate.

It's weird walking into the house without Mom there. She's been getting quieter over the last few months, paying less attention to us. It should have been a sign.

"God, I can't wait to clear out some of this crap," I tell Stan after I trip over a bat in the hallway, a remnant from my baseball days.

"Look at this," Stan says, kicking a pair of boots that he outgrew about ten years ago. "It won't take me long to throw my stuff in a backpack."

"Same here," I tell him.

Before I head to my room to pack, though, I wander over to the sofa with the permanent dent. I stare for a moment at the empty space Mom left behind. It's almost as if a part of her is still sitting there.

I'm dying for a good bash-out session with my drums, but they're still at Lu's place. I decide to stop there on the way over to Dad's.

The shadowy September dusk has settled in as I walk up the driveway towards Lu's side-door garage entrance. It's quiet on the street, so it's easy enough to hear low voices drifting out of Lu's yard. But these seem to be angry voices, or at least one, a woman's voice. Xing's voice? And she seems to be freaking out on Lu's dad.

"You keep coming home late, reeking of beer, Pete! It's not safe to drive like that. Hasn't it sunk in *yet*?"

Low mumbles from Lu's dad, then a slamming door. Oh man, what's going on?

I slink off into the darkness, heading toward Dad's place with all sorts of crazy thoughts spinning through my head. Does Lu even know about this? Where is she, anyway?

Then I remember: it's Monday night, and Lu isn't even home. She volunteers at the local community school on Monday evenings, helping with art lessons. So there's Lu, out banking her community service hours for high school. And there are her parents, having an argument about her dad's drinking habits out in the backyard.

Poor Lu, sitting on top of this and keeping

it all inside. No wonder she rolled her eyes when I talked about her perfect life. *Real perfect*, she said. How could I have missed it?

When I reach Dad and Josie's place a few minutes later, I find Josie, Dad, and Stan sitting at the kitchen table sipping hot cocoa and munching on home-baked cookies. There's a steaming mug waiting for me. I unleash a grateful smile on Josie as I sink into a chair.

"Thought this might take the edge off a rotten day," she tells me as she pushes the plate of cookies toward me.

"You can't even imagine." I take a quick sip of cocoa then reach for a chocolate chunk-dotted cookie. I smile around the table at this so-called family of mine.

By ten o'clock I'm so exhausted that I crawl between the nice crisp sheets of my nice firm bed in my nice clean room in this nice tidy house. Without even brushing my teeth! And I'm asleep before I can even remember to look at the Virago songbook.

13

ALMOST AWESOME

On Tuesday morning, Dad calls the hospital before he leaves for work. He finds out that Mom's tests have been delayed until later in the morning. Her doctor said to call back later for the results. The delay means I don't have to think about how serious it might be for a while longer, anyway.

It feels as if a couple of weeks have gone by instead of only twenty-four hours. At lunchtime I dig into the amazing lunch that Josie packed for me. My friends' faces register amazement as I sink my teeth into a tuna sub loaded down with veggies on a whole grain bun.

"Where did you *get* that?" Karim is practically drooling. "Can I *have* a bite?"

"I slept at my Dad's for a change last night," I tell him, avoiding the real explanation. "Josie made me lunch. And no, you can't have a bite."

"Your drums are still at my place, by the way," Lu reminds me.

"I know, and I miss them like crazy," I tell her. Definitely not a good time to mention what I overheard last night in her yard. Will there ever be one? "Karim, quit staring at my sub. I'll give you a cookie. I promise."

"So I put in a couple more of my community hours again last night, you guys." Lu arches an eyebrow. "Have you figured out how you'll be spending your forty hours' community service yet, Stelle?"

I cringe. I've been doing my best to avoid that subject. Haven't even banked any hours yet. "Does visiting my Nana at 'the home' count?"

"Maybe. What do you actually *do* there?"

Karim says. "I mean, when I volunteer at the food bank, I have to pack boxes with cans and sort stuff."

"Not much," I admit. "I just sort of sit there in a chair and stare at Nana. And try to think of stuff to talk about."

"Probably doesn't count," Lu says. Then she brightens. "But maybe if you do something else at the home — something that helps out with some of the other residents? I mean, if you're there anyway . . ."

"Sure! Spread some of the Stelle sunshine around a bit," Karim adds.

"Not a bad idea. I'll think about it. But first things first," I say, quickly changing the subject. "We need to get together for a practice soon, don't you think?" God, do I ever need the distraction of a jam session.

"Good idea," Lu says, then squints at me. "Too bad we don't have a lead singer yet though, huh?"

"Maybe we do. Guess what? This time I'm inviting Natalie for an audition."

Yep, it's true. I finally made up my mind to ask her. I still feel rotten about what happened on Monday with the Pink Girls. I just can't block out the image of her standing there dripping with cola in the hallway. And I can't forgive myself for not going to help her clean up. Lu grins and high fives me across the table.

"Yay for you, Stelle!" Karim says. When I look over, he's biting into the other half of my tuna sub.

That afternoon, between classes, I sidle up to Natalie at her locker and give her a quick nudge. When she sees it's me, she looks away, starts digging around through her stuff.

"Hey, Natalie. This Saturday at Lu's place. You up for it?" I ask, as if nothing happened between us.

Natalie slowly turns to face me. "Seriously?"

"Yeah. Let's give it a shot. Can you make it?"

Natalie's face breaks into a grin. "I'll be there," she says, then actually touches my arm. "Thanks, Stelle. And I'm sorry I went ballistic on you yesterday." She sighs. "It sucks to start every couple of years at a new school. It's way easier not to make friends, and just let people think I'm weird. In case we have to move again."

"Really?" I say, looking at her in a different way now, as if a light went on.

"Yup, really," she says. "I'm totally looking forward to Saturday, though. Should I bring my guitar?"

"Definitely — and any lyrics you want to try out," I tell her just as the bell rings and we both dash off in different directions. When I spot Lu walking ahead of me, I catch up and whisper, "We're on with Natalie," beside her ear. She gives me a thumbs-up. This is all working out very well. Finally!

Today is the best I've felt for a while. Maybe it's because Mom is actually in the care of medical professionals right now. Maybe it's because Josie is checking up on Nana today, so I don't have to worry about that so much either. Thank god for Josie.

I still have a huge load of other stuff on my mind though, like getting our house shovelled out while Mom's not there. Not to mention my school work, which has been suffering miserably over the past couple of weeks. And, ugh, trying to figure out my volunteer work and keep the guidance counsellor off my case. Today in the hallway she gave me the evil eye. So I spun around and walked the other way to avoid questions.

It still feels weird going home to Dad and Josie's place after school. When I walk through the door, I find Stan sitting at the kitchen table with Josie and they're sharing a laugh over something. There's a plate of muffins in front of him, and he's in the process of inhaling one that's slathered in melting butter.

"Banana chocolate chip," he says through a mouthful. "Still warm. Yum."

"Pull up a chair," Josie says. "I have some Nana news."

My stomach lurches a bit when she says that, and she pats my hand when I sink into the chair.

"Don't worry. It was just a bladder infection. Your Nana's on antibiotics now, and she was way better today. When I got there she wasn't even in her room — she was in someone else's, trying to walk off with a stuffed toy."

"Excellent!" I sigh with relief. "That means she's feeling better for sure."

"You know, we should take her out of there sometimes. It's such a depressing place. It would do her good."

"Where would we take her, Josie? Not to my Mom's place, that's for sure. I don't think either of them could handle it."

"You could bring her over here. I wouldn't mind. There's tons of room."

When I glance over at Stan, he's sitting there in mid-chew, staring at Josie.

"Are you *serious*?" he finally says.

"Of course. I don't mind at all."

"But what about Dad?" I'm a bit wary. "He'd mind, for sure."

"Doesn't matter. We share this house. So your Nana can stay in my half if he's not happy about it." Josie winks at me, yet again. "So now that we've got your Nana settled, we've got to sort out what's happening with your mom, right?"

When I look up Stan's eyes meet mine, then we both look over at Josie.

"All right, I'll make the phone call if you really want me to. I can understand how nervous you must be feeling about it," she tells us.

"Wow, you're *almost* awesome, Josie," Stan says, and Josie makes a face at him.

"You can't even imagine how much that *almost* means to me, Stan," she tells him, then reaches for the portable phone.

While Josie is on the phone, Stan and I

figure out a game plan. Josie has given us a pile of clear and green trash bags. We'll go over there right now and start working, so we can get rid of as much as possible before mom gets released from the hospital. Which could be sooner than we think, judging from the smile on Josie's face when she hangs up the phone.

"More good news. Your mom is fine, physically. It was just a slight concussion. A few other problems. They're trying out some medication on her, and having a psychiatrist in to speak to her. They said you can call her later to see if she's up to having visitors this evening."

"Okay, I guess we'll do that after supper," Stan finally says after we've stood there in silence for a moment. "Let's get moving on this, Stelle, before Mom gets home. That way she can start out fresh, sort of."

"Cool, Stan," I tell him. I love that now Stan seems to be taking charge of the situation. Finally, for the first time ever, I don't feel as if the entire burden is on me.

"Okay, guys, get moving on this mission of yours. Meanwhile I'll whip up something for dinner. I think I have some homemade pasta sauce in the freezer. See you back here around 6:30."

"My stomach heard you," Stan says. "It's already grumbling."

14

STUCK INSIDE OF ME

When we walk in, the place is strangely silent. It's almost as though our house is holding its breath, waiting to find out what will happen next — kind of like Stan and me. There's the familiar stench of old shoes just inside the front door. I can hear a tap dripping somewhere. In the roaring silence it almost sounds like a drumbeat.

"We need music," I tell Stan. In a few seconds I've tuned into a noisy rock station on the radio that helps to drown out the emptiness. "Ah, much better. Let's do this, Stan."

We start by filling the huge blue bin and

some clear recycling bags with newspapers and magazines, And all those empty boxes that Mom said she might use to wrap presents in some day. Store receipts and shopping lists on torn envelopes, and tons of junk mail and brochures. Used gift wrap all refolded and waiting to never be used again, all stacked up in disarray waiting to be discarded by us. It's such a relief to unload the bags through the front door and down to the curb.

After an hour we take a soda break and admire our handiwork. The surfaces are almost all cleared away now, except for the teetering stacks of books everywhere.

"We're getting there," Stan says. "I'm tossing out all those old boots and shoes in the front hall now. They totally reek! Then I'm going to start filling bags with old clothes and stuff to drop off at Goodwill. Should we get rid of the books?"

"God, no. She *loves* her books. Maybe we can find some cheap bookcases at Ikea or something and set them up in her bedroom this weekend. I'm getting started on the kitchen now. Flinging all the expired stuff. How did we put up with this for so long, anyway?"

"Guess we just ignored it."

"Sort of the way we ignored Mom?" I can't help adding.

"Look, she didn't do anything to help herself, Stelle. And we did what we could to keep this house functional. Don't start trying to blame us for her problems."

"Ugh. I can't believe we let it get this bad." I take a sip of cola and savour the fizzy burn in my throat. "Why didn't we do this a long time ago?"

"Because she wouldn't *let* us! We tried, remember? And she freaked out any time we suggested it. So we let it go. It's not our fault."

"I just hope she doesn't freak out when she gets home and all the stuff's gone!"

"Hopefully she'll be well medicated by then," Stan says, wrinkling his nose as he opens the fridge. "I think she's got a lot of psychological junk to work out, too. So getting rid of all this clutter can only help her, right?"

We don't even notice how much time has passed until the phone rings to remind us. We've totally forgotten about dinner. I don't realize how starved I am until I'm sitting in Josie's dining room, twirling the first forkful of pasta. Dad's going around the table with some sort of gourmet parmesan cheese grinder, grating fresh cheese over our steaming plates. And they've even served us red wine in long-stemmed crystal goblets!

I swear I've died and gone to heaven. And I feel a little pang of guilt when I catch myself wishing that they might keep Mom in the hospital for a while longer. Then I remember that we have to call her after dinner, and the thought of it makes me practically choke on a huge mouthful of noodles . . .

"Hi, Mom. It's Stelle. You okay?"

"Getting there, honey. Hope to be coming home soon."

"Well, guess what. There's a surprise

waiting for you when you get here. We got rid of all the crap in the house that you've been saving the last couple of years. It's gone now. We flung it all."

"You what? I told you I needed that stuff, didn't I? I'm going to kill myself now, Stelle."

Click.

Okay, so that's a 'worst case scenario'. But I can't stop thinking about it as I'm dialling the hospital number.

"Hello?"

My stomach twists. "Is that you, Mom?" I whisper.

"Yes, it's me, Stelle. You okay? I can barely hear you."

"Am *I* okay? Why do you keep asking me that, Mom? I found *you* on the floor, remember?"

"That's why I'm asking *you*, Stelle. That must have been awful for you."

Mom's voice, sounding weak and shaky, gives away her ordeal. But she sounds more sensible now than she has in months. She's not shrieking, she's not whining, she's not bitching. She's just talking in a nearly normal voice that I almost think I can remember from a quite a few years ago.

"Yeah, I guess it *was* awful. I thought you were dead."

"Not yet, Stelle. You don't think you can get rid of me that easily, do you?" she says with a low chuckle.

I don't know whether to laugh or cry.

Mom decides she's not up to having company tonight. She has a bit of a headache and just feels like going to sleep. Maybe tomorrow.

"Don't take it personally, Stelle. Your mom's still recovering," Josie says when I hang up. "She needs to get lots of rest."

"I'm okay with it." Stan shrugs. "I'm not sure if I'm ready to see her anyway. I'm not even sure I'll know what to say when I *do* see her."

"How can you say something like that?" I yelp.

"Because it's true, Stelle. What are *you* going to say? How's it going, Mom? How are they treating you here? What kind of meds did they put you on, anyway? By the way, are you crazy, or what?"

"God, Stan. You really are such a jerk sometimes."

"Well it's true, isn't it? What *are* you going to say to her?"

"'How are you feeling' would be a good start."

"You're kidding, right? It's a totally redundant question, isn't it?"

"No it *isn't*, and you're a totally redundant ass, Stan."

"Whoa." Dad holds up his hands. "You two have *got* to start watching the language around here." He points at Josie's belly and she rubs it and nods.

"Whatever, Dad. I've got some studying to do." Stan goes stalking off to his room and leaves me and Josie and Dad standing there staring at one another.

"Guess he has a point," I admit. "Thanks for the great dinner, Josie. And for the great parmesan, Dad." Josie chuckles her approval. "I've got to work on an essay now."

As I head for my room I try to ignore the surge of relief I'm feeling at the thought that we've gotten a reprieve from facing our mom. At least for today, anyway.

I don't really have an essay to write. I finished it in study hall at school today. I want to check out Mom's songbook again, maybe try to make some sense from her lyrics.

What I'm most impressed with is that my mom totally nailed the whole songwriting structure and technique. Besides the verses and chorus, her songs even include a bridge, a sort of a song summary that takes you back to the beginning. I can't ever seem to come up with a good bridge for my songs, so I usually just skip it. I can't suppress a little twang of jealousy because her songs are actually way better than mine!

The one that grabs me the most is called *Stuck Inside of Me*. It's such a sad and desperate ballad. I can't help wondering what happened that compelled her to write it.

There's just no denying it,
This dream's a part of me now,
not so sure if that's good or bad,
but I'll pull it off somehow.

The world isn't buying it,
but I know it's part of me now,
They think this dream is just a fad,
But I'll prove them wrong somehow.

Chorus:
What's stuck deep inside of me,
has taken on a life of its own,
What's stuck deep inside of me
Should melt your heart of stone, stone, stone . . .

Bridge:
I'll never part with the dream in my heart

yeah, I really think you should know that . . .

I like this song a lot. I practically have it memorized by the time I turn out my light. But what has me completely confused is the why of it. After all, Mom has always been so stuck on making sure that Stan and I took music lessons. Clearly she thinks that there's something important about music.

Why is she so in denial about music when she wrote such good songs? And had her own band? If it were me, I'd be bragging about it to my kids. How cool, to sing in a girl band. It's my dream!

A while later as I'm trying to fall asleep, a melody keeps looping through my thoughts. And I realize that I've already put my mom's hypnotic words to music.

15

THAT SINKING FEELING

On Wednesday evening Mom is ready to see us. But are we ready to see her? Now that I've read Mom's songs, I feel as though I've peered through a keyhole into her poor messed-up head. So the truth is, I'm actually looking forward to seeing her today.

In the car on the way to the hospital, the three of us ride along in complete silence. Dad waits out in the parking lot as Stan and I walk through the hallways like we're on our way to our own executions. We both stop in front of her door.

"You go ahead," Stan whispers. "She only wanted to see *you* on Monday."

"Chicken." I walk through the doorway alone.

Mom is half-sitting up in her bed, still wearing her hospital gown. She still has an IV line stuck in her hand. I can already tell that she has a bit more colour now. But when she turns her face in my direction, she looks less than thrilled to see me.

"Hi, Mom."

"You made it, huh, Stelle?"

"Yup. How are you feeling?"

She turns her face away from me and stares out the window.

"What's it like outside?" Her voice is a dull monotone.

"Warm. For the end of September. Um. When are you coming home?"

"Pretty soon. Tomorrow or the next day." Her voice is beginning to tremble. "I feel like crap, Stelle. They told me this medication could take a while to kick in."

"What is it anyway, Mom?"

"Antidepressants. Apparently I'm depressed."

She's still not looking at me. But I can see enough of her cheek to spot the tears that are leaking out now in a sad, slow trickle. God, she looks awful with her tangled hair and slack face.

"Is there anything I can do to help, Mom?"

She sighs. "I don't know, Stelle. All I know is that I'm terrified of going back to that house. All that crap everywhere." She swipes at her tears. "I'm just so sorry about all this." Then she looks at me. "You told the doctor about the house, didn't you? All my stuff being everywhere."

"I had to, Mom. I just want you to get better, that's all. So I told him the truth." My throat starts to tighten. "Stan's waiting outside in the hall."

"Call him in, Stelle."

"Stan!"

He peers around the corner. I can read the terror on his face.

"It's okay. Mom wants to see you. She won't bite, will you, Mom?" When I glance over at

Mom, she hasn't even tried to smile. I wish I could somehow snatch back those words in midair before they reach her ears. Stan shuffles into the room, staring at the floor.

"Hi, Stan," she says without looking at him.

"Hi, Mom. Did Stelle tell you what we did?"

Crap! What is his *problem*? It's too soon! I shoot a frantic look his way so he'll shut up before she starts asking questions. But it's too late. She heard him and she's looking at us now.

"No, she didn't, Stan. *What* did you do?"

"Um. It's a surprise. For when you get home, Mom." Stan tries to smile but it melts away on his face. "When *are* you coming home?"

"Soon, Stan. And I'm not really in the mood for surprises. So you might as well tell me what you did right now. You didn't burn the house down, did you? "

Stan looks at me, his eyes pleading for help. I have to come to his rescue.

"Well as a matter of fact, Stan and I kind of took a stab at de-cluttering and got rid of some of, well, some of the . . . um . . . *excess* for you. We thought maybe we were doing you a favour."

"But you didn't even ask me first, Stelle. Why would you do that?"

Uh-oh. Not the response we were hoping for.

Then Stan pipes up. "So you wouldn't have to face it when you come home. And besides. It's dangerous. It's actually a fire hazard." Yay, Stan!

"And the paramedics had a hard time wading through it to rescue you on Monday, Mom," I add. "It really isn't safe to have all that junk clogging up the hallways and doorways."

"But what if I *need* it?" Her chin is trembling now and her voice is rising. She starts to sniffle. "What if I *need* some of that stuff, Stelle?" She reaches out one of her plump hands and clasps my wrist.

"We kept all your books," Stan murmurs as he begins backing out of the room. I'd like to be doing the same thing, but Mom won't let go of my wrist. She's starting to freak me out. I'm afraid she might start shaking and crying uncontrollably again.

And then a nurse breezes in and rescues me. She senses Mom's distress, and I'm pretty sure she senses mine, too.

"Everything okay in here?" she asks. "Visiting hours are just about over." She gently unwraps Mom's fingers from my wrist and applies a blood pressure cuff to her arm. "Let's just see how you're doing, okay?" The nurse smiles at me in a practiced, efficient way and continues what she's doing. "This is your daughter, isn't it? And your son's in the doorway?"

Mom nods and sniffles as the nurse pumps the bulb then starts releasing the air from the cuff.

"We'd better say goodnight," I tell her, then motion to Stan behind my back.

We both kiss her forehead then slink out of her room.

"Rats deserting a sinking ship," Stan says as we scuffle along the hall towards the exit and freedom.

I feel lame, too, as if we're just abandoning her there, with her tear-stained face and rumpled hair and thin hospital gown. This state she's reached has been a long time coming. I have a sinking feeling that it'll be a long time going, too.

16

NOBODY'S FAULT

With so much on my mind, school days have started to become school *daze*. By Thursday I feel as if I'm simply going through the motions but not really participating. Part of me is someplace else, preoccupied with things that I never could have imagined a few weeks ago. I haven't touched my drums for days. At lunchtime, everyone keeps asking me what's wrong, and I don't even have the energy to choke out an answer.

After school on Thursday, I decide to suck it up and visit with Nana, even though it's not my regular visiting day. I need to see that she's okay after last week, even if Josie has been there to check on her.

At least she's dressed when I get there. At least she's sitting in her chair, instead of in a puddle in her bed. She's holding a random stuffed toy, though, so some poor inmate must be missing theirs.

"Where'd you get that?" I peck her paper-dry cheek, pat her crumpled hands.

"Wally brought it. He came to see me today."

What? *Dad* came here? "He did, Nana? When?"

"I can't remember. After lunch? Or was it after breakfast? Or after lunch?"

Poor Nana. She's so confused. There's no way Dad would have shown up here today. The nice nurse swishes in behind me.

"Oh, hi, Stelle. Nana is doing so much better today, aren't you, Mrs. Draper?" She hands Nana a tiny paper cup. "Pill time." Nana obediently pops the pill into her mouth and takes a gulp of water. "Did she tell you your dad was in today, Stelle?"

"He really *was*?"

"This morning. He brought her a stuffed cat. And told her he hopes she'll be in purr-fect condition again soon. It was sweet." The nurse smiles. "Nice guy, your dad. And handsome, too."

"Wait a minute. *My* dad did all this."

"He *told* me he was your dad, so unless he was lying, and was just some random stranger dropping in . . . well, you get my drift." The nurse swishes right back out again.

"Wow. You're kidding me." I stand there shaking my head. Nana's staring at me now. Her small dark eyes are like raisins pushed into a big oatmeal cookie.

"I told you Wally was here today, Donna. Why don't you ever believe me?"

Oh no. Not again. I don't even have the energy to correct her.

"He's such a lovely man, Wally is, Donna. I know he's exactly what you need."

"Pardon, Nana? What are you *talking* about?"

"You already know damned well it would be a huge mistake for you to take off. Why you would *ever* want to break up with him is beyond me. Just for that silly dream of yours."

"What. Silly. Dream?"

"Nothing will ever come of it. You're just not good enough." She shakes her head and clucks and fusses with her covers. "As for lending you the money to go, that is out of the question. I know I'll never see a red cent of it again anyway. It's simply not worth it . . ."

Mom's song.

"Nana, please stop." I feel like plugging my ears.

"You're sticking with Wally, Donna. He's a nice boy, and at least you'll have a stable life here. At least you won't wind up disappointed when you take off for Los Angeles and get *nowhere*."

"*Nana*! Please stop talking. Be *quiet*!"

I actually do plug my ears. Her mouth keeps moving, though.

I sink slowly to the edge of Nana's bed.

What did my mom actually give up to become Donna Czulinski, a wife and mother? Did Nana and Dad *make* her do it? And is there still a Virago Girl stuck somewhere deep inside of who she's become?

———

Later that evening, lying on my bed, I find myself staring at a spider on the ceiling, wishing I could trade places with it. Because now I understand. Now I get the meaning of Mom's song. And I think I'm also starting to get the meaning of my Mom.

Donna Draper had a dream of making music and seeing how far she could take it, and Nana totally crushed it.

What's stuck deep inside of me / has taken on a life of its own / What's stuck deep inside of me / Should melt your heart of stone, stone, stone . . .

My poor mom.

"Stelle? Dinner's ready!" Josie's voice ricochets up the stairs and finds me on the bed.

They're all sitting around the table when I get there, a circle of almost happy-looking faces, about to plunge their forks into a home-made shepherd's pie. It almost makes me feel like smiling myself.

"So you'll never guess who I went to see today, Stelle," Dad says as soon as I sit down. He looks like he's about to split wide open, while Josie just seems perplexed.

"You never told me you went to see anyone today, Wally," she says.

"I was saving it as a surprise. I went to see your *Nana*, Stelle. At the nursing home."

"You *did*? That was sweet, honey." Josie squeezes his hand. "You're going to make such an amazing new daddy."

"I know, Dad. The nurse told me you were there. She said you're 'hot'. Well, maybe not those exact words, but she suggested it."

"She did?" Dad's practically beaming now. So are Stan and Josie.

"No kidding," Stan says. "So was she holding a white cane or what?"

Josie breaks up and Dad glares at Stan.

"It was nice of you to go there today, Dad. I think Nana appreciated your visit."

"You mean she mentioned it? She knew who I was?"

"Oh yeah, I'm pretty sure she knew *exactly* who you were. Seeing your face after so long probably jolted her memory. She sure said some weird things. When she thought I was Mom."

His face freezes and he looks at me funny for a second.

"I found out about Mom's band. About Virago Girls. I saw your old yearbooks. From down in the crawlspace. And . . . well . . ."

Stan and Josie are staring at me now. But Dad is staring into his plate.

"And well what, Stelle?" he murmurs.

"And I know about Mom's major dream. Of taking off for LA. She even wrote a song about it. So why did Nana kill her dream?"

"What the *hell*?" Stan says, and Josie quietly places her hand on top of his.

Dad is looking at us now. His face is sheepish. "Okay, kids, there's a whole bunch you don't know about your mom and me. For one thing, she was one hot, rocking chick when she was Stelle's age."

"*Huh*?" Stan says, then looks at me and frowns. "Why didn't you tell me all this stuff before, Stelle?"

"Because I just figured it all out myself," I tell him. "Nana kind of blabbed some stuff. When she thought I was Mom."

Dad clears his throat. "I was crazy about her and I didn't want her to leave. So it became a little conspiracy between your Nana and me. She held back the money. And I talked Donna out of going. Bloody selfish, I guess?"

"Oh, Wally," Josie whispers.

"The crazy, ironic part is that by keeping her here, I lost her anyway. She always felt sort of ripped off and resentful about having to settle for something she didn't really want. Is it any wonder it all fell apart?" Dad rakes his fingers through his hair and sighs.

"Don't even blame yourself, Dad," I tell him. "Or Nana. Because it's nobody's fault."

Then I do it. Reach across the table and squeeze my dad's big hand. And he squeezes mine right back.

17

TRULY COOL

Our mom is like the walking dead. When we brought her home this morning and she climbed out of the car, she moved as if she was walking through water.

Thank god it's Saturday, so Dad was able to pick her up. But she never even uttered a word while he drove, just sat hunched beside me in the back. When she stepped through the front door she stopped and sucked in her breath. The sight of the tidy kitchen made her face sort of crumple. She sank into her pre-squashed sofa cushion, folded into herself and started to sob.

She's still there, lying down now. I've brought pillows from her bedroom so she'll be more comfortable. It's past noon and she won't eat or even have a sip of her liquid nutritional supplement. I don't know what to do with her.

Out in the kitchen, Stan's making grilled cheese. A fully functional kitchen that we can finally use the way it was meant to be used. Mom hasn't spoken a word to us yet, except to tell us she's sorry for burdening us like this. And that she's pretty sure that she'll never be hungry again in this lifetime.

Every time I look at my Mom, it's as if I'm trying to find that slim girl in the tight black dress. That Virago Girl who's buried underneath all the sadness and angst. The one who wrote such amazing songs and performed on stage in front of her school. The girl with the dream that died, and killed her spirit along with it.

It's a relief to get out of the house and escape from the burden of a mom who's saddled with mental illness. Stan has promised to keep an eye on her while I head over to our band practice.

It's gorgeous out today. The sun massages my head and lights up the early autumn treetops like lanterns. There's almost a sort of hope in the air. I hear a shout from behind me and spin around. Natalie is floating towards me like a crinoline cloud, her guitar flung over her shoulder. I wait for her to catch up.

"I'm so looking forward to this," she says, flicking ashes from a cigarette. "Snagged this butt from my mom's purse. She actually thinks that nobody knows she smokes! Thanks for inviting me, Stelle."

This feels good, me and her walking side by side toward a Saturday jam session. And I think it's time for me to finally ask what I've been wondering since the first time I ever saw her.

"Can I ask you something I've been curious about?" Then I say it before I can lose my nerve. "Why do you dress that way, Nat?"

"What way?" She half laughs then flicks her butt down a sewer grate. "I dunno. There's just something I like about it. The statement, I guess. Because I sure don't want to be one of those pink girls." I laugh when she says that. "And I sure don't want to be like you or Lu, either."

My laugh gets stuck like a piece of hard candy in my throat. "*Pardon me?*"

"No offense or anything."

"Offense *taken*," I huff. "And what's that supposed to *mean*, anyway?"

"Oh, Stelle, don't have a hissy fit, okay? I just try to avoid normalcy. But the truth is, underneath all this 'stuff' I'm wearing, the clothes, the piercings, the hair, and makeup, sadly, I really am only ordinary." She shakes her head and her earrings tinkle.

"Well, I wouldn't go quite that far," I tell her with a nervous laugh. Natalie — *ordinary*? How can she even *think* that?

"Same with the rest of my family. One daughter, *moi*, one son away at college. CEO dad who's always getting job transfers. Math tutor mom who's always selling the wonders of math. I honestly wish I could be more 'out there'." She actually sounds wistful.

When I look over, she's wearing a twisted smile. "Are you *kidding* me?" I say.

"Nope. My folks are so busy, they barely notice when I dress like this. But everyone at school does. And they all keep their distance. Which works for me."

"So you dress weird to make people nervous. And won't change your style even when the pink girls bully you because if it." I shake my head. "And wish you could be more 'out there'? That's wild."

"Yeah, I know," she says raising one eyebrow. "I mean, sometimes I feel like a freakin' poseur. But if I could be part of your band, now that would be *truly* cool."

This girl is more of an enigma than ever now. I mean, at home she wants to be noticed — hence the get-up — but wants to be left alone — also, hence the get-up?

Maybe 'ordinary' really is all relative. And maybe crazy is too.

———

As it turns out, Natalie really is freaking cool. She's just played us one of her own songs in Lu's garage. Something quirky about how you have to lose yourself before you can really find yourself. That strange quivering thing she can do with her voice is killer! Plus she has great range. The girl totally *is* out there! She just hasn't realized it yet.

"That was . . . oh, wow, Nat," Lu says, just shaking her head.

"Awesome song," I tell her. "We need to cover it."

Karim is just about losing it himself, he's so impressed. "Your voice kills it, and your style just blows me away. I want to shop Value Village with you! You rock!"

Nat just stands there smiling in an almost shy way. "You're all nuts," she says.

Lu's still grinning like mad.

"Holy crap. We've finally got a band," she says. "Now all we need is a name."

Karim has a wild look in his eye. He takes little sip from the flask he smuggled in his back-pack, and makes a happy smacking sound before passing it off to Natalie. "How about *Virago*?"

"What? You mean like my mom's band back in the '80s?"

"Why not? It's a cool name. Anyway, they were Virago *Girls*, weren't they?"

"Wait. Your mom had a *band*, Stelle? Impressive. That's *way* beyond ordinary." Nat shoots me a knowing smile. Hah! If only she knew about the *rest* of it. "And Virago. What a great name."

"I guess that could work," I say.

"I *love* that!" Lu has picked up her own guitar. "So now we have two electric guitars and two percussionists. Too bad we don't have someone to play bass guitar."

"I have a bass guitar," Nat says. "I can play both."

We're all staring at her now like three slack-jawed fools. This girl has talent. Lu has printed out booklets of our songs and we give her one. While she leafs through it, I sit on my throne and pick up my sticks for the first time in over a week. It feels so awesome to be sitting there again. I try a few noisy solos on the bass drum and ride cymbal to get back into the swing of it.

Whenever I play my drums, I get into the 'zone', where nothing else in the world matters. It's happening right now. Eyes squeezed shut, pounding and crashing, and flinging my head around as if I'm half-crazed. Punctuating the thumps and clashes with a few well-timed yelps and shrieks. When I finally stop to catch my breath and open my eyes, my three friends are staring at me as if I really am crazy.

"Are you totally losin' it or what, girl?" Karim says.

"Lately, I'm not even sure any more," I admit.

Afterwards I set out for home, walking along with Natalie for a while. Maybe I need to get Karim to take me treasure hunting, as he calls it. I feel so drab and *non*-groovy around this girl. Then she turns off in the direction of her street and I'm alone with my thoughts, trying to stay positive after such an epic rehearsal.

As soon as my house is in sight, my spirits begin to plummet. The good news is that Stan has finally mowed the lawn, which was starting to look like a hayfield.

Mom's still parked on the sofa, but what else did I expect? The TV is turned on, and I can't decide if that's a good sign or a bad one. At least she's actually watching something. It's only the Weather Network, but it's a start. Then she really surprises me.

"Hi, Stelle."

Lately Mom *never* addresses me first, so I'm actually shocked. "Uh . . . hi, Mom. So? What's new?" I cringe as soon as the words are out.

Mom's head swivels slowly. One eyebrow

has shifted upward just a little, as if she sees the irony in my question.

"CityTV called a few minutes ago. They invited me to appear on *Fashion Friday*." Her eyes open wide.

And I laugh out loud because it really is kind of funny, just the thought of my mom in her current state strutting her stuff on TV. Then she says something else that surprises me.

"Get me one of those chalky strawberry supplements, Stelle. And take the bottle of my antidepressants out of my overnight case, okay?"

"Sure, Mom." And I do it, right away, before she can change her mind.

The plastic bottle of orange capsules says *apo-something-or-other* on the label. There's a prescription for thirty days, with two repeats. I set it in plain sight. Then I snap open the tab on the supplement can and pour it into a glass with ice cubes. I add a straw. That's when I decide to put some cheese and crackers on a plate.

I set a tray with Mom's 'meal' on the coffee table beside her. She pokes at a piece of cheese as if it's some alien substance.

"Thanks, sweetie." She looks right into my eyes. "And thanks for cleaning this place up. I really appreciate it." She starts to blink quickly, as if she's about to cry. "I mean. I'm still freaked out, but I get it. I was completely paralyzed, Stelle — couldn't even face it. I thanked Stan before he left."

"I thought he was in his room. He left?" He left her here *alone*? In this condition? He knew I had a band practice, the jerk.

"I *told* him to, Stelle. I told him I'd be fine. Every time I looked up he was in the doorway staring at me with these worried eyes."

Okay, so maybe he's not such a jerk after all.

Should I try to extinguish my sudden spark of hope? Is she really going to give this a shot and try to get better?

I don't care. I'm getting my own hopes up. I plop down on the sofa beside my mom and nibble on a piece of cheese as she sips her supplement and makes a yucky face. The repeating loop of weather news is starting to make me crazy, and I pick up the converter.

"Do you mind if I flip around a bit? See what's on?" I ask her. My mom just shakes her head and waves at the TV.

I start flipping through the higher channels, stop briefly on MuchRetro, one of the digital stations that Dad pays for, then keep channel surfing.

"Wait!" Mom says. "Go back there for a sec."

"Back where?" I don't want to assume, but does she really mean MuchRetro?

"That was Annie Lennox. God, I used to love her."

My finger can't move fast enough. When I land on the channel, Annie Lennox and the Eurythmics are rocking "Sweet Dreams" in the original music video. It is ultra cool. I've always loved those lyrics myself. A virago song if there ever was one.

"You have no idea how much I wanted to be that virago girl," Mom murmurs.

My mom looks distant, wistful. It almost gives me hope.

18

WHAT MIGHT HAVE BEEN

Mom didn't eat the cheese and crackers. But at least she finished the shake. And I ate the cheese and crackers.

Now Mom is fixated on my laptop that's set up on the coffee table in front of her. And she's been grinning ever since I hooked her up with YouTube, and we found a bunch of old '80s music videos of her favourite bands. I'm pretty sure she's totally enjoying this blast from the past.

I've learned a lot about her taste in music, too, that she used to love Roxette, and Patti Smith, and Chrissie Hynde and the Pretenders, and Siouxsie and the Banshees.

I decide to do something that's probably the complete opposite of what I should be doing. But this needs to come out.

"Mom?" I turn to face her, sit cross-legged on the sofa. "I'm glad you finished your shake."

"I wish I could be hungrier. Thanks for the cheese and crackers." She reaches out her hand and squeezes mine. Her fingernails are clean now. Even her hair looks better, falling in a soft veil around her face. I can see how she was actually quite pretty once. I squeeze her hand back.

I take a deep breath. "Mom, can I sing something for you?"

"Like what? Something you wrote for your band?"

"*What?*"

"Stelle, I might have *seemed* catatonic all this time, but I'm not stupid. The *drumsticks* you left on your desk! The finger drumming on every surface. The way you head over to your dad's all the time. I figured you were playing the drums. And that you probably have a kit at Wally and Josie's place."

"Oh. But the band. How did you find out . . ."

"Stan blew your cover. I asked him where you were this afternoon. That was when he mentioned you were over at Lu's jamming in her garage. Then, of course, he slapped his forehead. And told me everything."

Stupid Stan! "Are you okay with that, Mom?"

"A while back I might not have been, but right now nothing fazes me. And anyway, Stelle, what's so bad about having a band?" She looks at me as if she can read my thoughts. "You know, don't you," she says. "About Virago Girls? You found my yearbooks. And my songbook. I saw them on your bed."

"Yeah. They were in the crawlspace. I've been reading your songs. I love them."

My mom looks surprised for an instant. "You do?"

"Yeah. They're really good. Even better

than the ones I write. I'd like for our band to cover a couple of them."

"You *would*?" Her face suddenly lights up. And I think, yes, I'm sure of it, Mom is actually smiling, and it's a *real* smile! "Which ones, Stelle?"

"Well, I love *Aching to be Free.*"

There's a distant look on her face, as if she's spotted something from long ago in her mind's eye. "Oh wow. *That* one? Talk about a blast from the past. I was trying to ditch some guy."

"Figured that. But my favourite one is . . ." Should I say it? "*Stuck Inside of Me.* Do you remember *that* one Mom?"

"You know, *don't* you," she whispers, and I nod.

"Why didn't you tell me about your band, and your dreams? Like, a long time ago?"

Mom dabs at her nose. It looks sore. "I don't know. I guess I just couldn't talk about it. It's been choking me for like twenty years."

"But it would have explained so much. About

you *and* Dad. About why it didn't work out."

Her head turns slowly and she sucks in a deep breath. "I've made a lot of mistakes, Stelle. But you and Stan are the gift that makes up for everything I *might have* missed out on. I couldn't let you think I've resented you, just because it turned out this way."

If she'd taken off to live her dream, we might never have been born. Whoa. She probably loves us like crazy and resents us like crazy at the same time.

"So what made you go looking through the crawlspace?" she asks. "Not enough junk to keep you busy on the main floor?" There's a shadow of an ironic smile on her face that's nice to see.

This is probably the perfect time to tell her about Nana. In music they'd call it a segue. And that's how the rest of my Saturday night plays itself out. And it's absolutely awful, because after I fill my mom in about Nana's condition and how she thinks that I'm 'Donna', I finally get to hear the entire sordid story from start to finish.

At my age she was experimenting with drugs, partying madly, and dreaming big. It got so bad that Nana started to associate music with Mom's sketchy lifestyle. Figured that was why she was acting reckless and causing so much grief for her. So in the end Nana conspired with Wally, the guy from drama class who loved her madly. And Mom wound up staying home to raise a family.

"And I guess it's finally time to admit that the outcome was mostly my fault, Stelle. I mean, what did I expect, breaking all the rules every chance I could? Maybe if I'd pursued music in a more serious way, it would have turned out differently." Mom's nose twitches and she rubs her face. "So in the end, I cut off my nose to spite my face."

I frown at her and tip my head. "Huh? What does that even mean?"

"Well, I took it out on everyone including myself, but in the end, I just hurt myself the most. Look at all the years I've wasted, missing out on music. And on forcing a classical instrument on kids who are basically rockers. I've missed out on a good relationship with my mother, too." She blows out a long sigh. "And now it's too bloody late."

She explains how, as we were growing up, she didn't want us getting into drugs and partying the way she did. That was why she insisted that Stan and I take the 'stupid violin', as she put it, to try to protect us or lead us along a safer path or something. And she's never stopped wondering what 'might have been' if she'd acted less irresponsibly and been allowed to chase her dream.

The only thing I can do is listen until she's finished talking, and is completely spent from the effort. Afterwards we sit in silence for a couple of hours. We don't bother to turn on any lights. Dusk slides in, fills the living room with a smudgy grey that reflects the way we're both feeling. We sit nestled on the sofa, arms around each other's shoulders until the darkness settles on us like a woollen blanket.

19

LET IT GO

Sunday is quiet. Mom is quiet on the sofa. We talk a little, mostly sit in silence. When I tune into MuchRetro again, she asks me to please turn it off for now. I scramble some eggs, nice and fluffy, with cheese melted on top, try to tempt her to eat some. But no. She manages to swallow a can of liquid supplement. Stan finishes off the eggs then heads for his job at the video store. And I'm left alone with Mom again.

I do my best to hide the fact that I'm exhausted from everything that's happened this week. I feel like crawling under my covers and hiding there for a long time. But like a good daughter/granddaughter, I don't. I call the home to see how Nana is, and they say she's fine today, up to her old tricks. I pass that message on to Mom, who just stares into space, frowning when I tell her.

It's completely overwhelming. I need to escape from the suffocation of mom's state of mind. So I hide in my room for a while and try to write something.

Let It Go

You've lost yourself, you've slipped away
I seem to know you less each day
that haunted look behind your eyes
that mask you wear, that thin disguise

I try to do my best, I try to let you know,
Each day I dream, I wish, I pray
That somehow you will find a way
To let it go, let it go, just let it go.

Not great, but it's a start, and it explains the way I feel. How I wish she could just leave that part of her life behind and get on with the rest of it.

"So, when are you going to sing me the song, Stelle?"

I spin around in my desk chair. Mom's standing in my bedroom doorway, looking at me. Is it my imagination or does she actually seem thinner, as if part of her has melted away over the last little while?

"What song, Mom?"

"The one you were going to sing to me yesterday, just before we both fell asleep on the sofa. You know, the one . . . about . . ." She brushes a wisp of hair off her face and watches me.

"Are you sure Mom? Maybe it's not such a good idea, to sing it right now.."

She lets out a snort. "I like to think of this as therapy. Don't look surprised. The doctor says I have to get past my past, and how else am I going to do it?" She grimaces. "So whenever you're ready, hit it."

"Wow, Mom, you're amazing." I can't

resist the impulse to jump out of my chair and hug her. "You're gonna be okay, you know. After all, you *are* the original virago girl!"

Mom looks surprised for a moment then one eyebrow pops up.

"Yeah, I guess I am." Then she hugs me back. "I love your optimism, sweetie." She gingerly touches the spot where she bashed her head. "This bump hardly hurts anymore when I press on it." She winces.

"Don't press on it, Mom! Bend down. Show me the spot."

Mom leans over and points to the bump. "I like to think of it as my wake-up call," Her hair is hanging over her face, but I can almost hear her smile.

I rub my fingertips over it gently and shudder. "Ouch. That musta hurt!"

When Mom stands up again she really is smiling. "I don't remember. It knocked me out. Hurt like hell after though!"

I snicker when she says that, because I can't help it, then I cover my mouth. Come to think of it, my Mom's pretty funny when she wants to be.

"It's okay to laugh, Stelle. Honest. I think I've missed it over the years."

"We've all missed it, Mom. Even Dad has, I'm sure."

She shrugs. "That's likely one of the oh-so-many reasons that he left." She sighs and drags her fingers through her hair, pushing away her bangs. Now I have a perfect view of her forlorn eyes. "God, I was a fool for so long, wasn't I?"

"You couldn't help it," I whisper, then squeeze her shoulder. "You were sick. I feel so lame for not being able to help you more. Honestly, I'm so sorry about that, Mom."

"Sweetie, how could you help me when you didn't even know what my problem was? I feel lame for never telling you about it." She shakes her head. "I want to show you something the doctor gave me. Wait right here, okay?"

Mom shuffles to her room. I wait. A minute

later she's pressing a crumpled piece of paper into my hand.

"It's a sort of prescription. Read it out loud," she says with a small smile.

She's handed me a slip of paper from a doctor's prescription pad. His name is at the top. But the only thing scribbled on the paper is '*Be gentle with yourself*'. I read it out loud, twice.

Then I frown and look at my mom. "Your doctor wrote this?"

"Uh huh. I've been keeping it close by ever since. I look at it every now and then. Just to remind myself."

I squeeze her warm, soft hand.

"And when I forget, because I just might, please remind me, Stelle. Okay?"

"Okay, Mom," I tell her. And then she walks away before I can even sing her the song.

After Stan gets home from work, we order

Swiss Chalet and hope she'll at least be tempted by fries dipped in that awesome sauce. She actually picks one fry up, dips it into the sauce, and licks it off. Then she half-smiles.

"That almost tastes good. Sure wish I felt hungrier." She drops the fry and stares off into space again.

"Maybe it's just because of the medication . . ." Stan offers, then his voice peters out. She's clearly thinking about something else now.

"Tell me about Josie." Mom has never asked that question until this very moment. "What's their house like? Do you like her? Will she be a good mom?"

"Huh?" Stan doesn't even try to hide his bewilderment.

"Well . . . um . . ." is the only response I can find at first. Mom's eyes are wider and clearer than they've been in ages. "You *really* want to know?"

"That's why I asked, Stelle."

So we tell her, answering all her questions

honestly. Mom listens with her elbow on the table, her chin perched on her hand. Laughs a bit when I use the Martha Stewart analogy. Then we tell her how helpful Josie has been over the past week, how kind and understanding.

As we tidy up the kitchen the conversation continues, the three of us focusing entirely on one another. We talk about how much our lives have changed since Dad left, and how we're all learning to cope in our own ways. Mom even adds the word 'finally' when she talks about herself, then wistfully strokes the lump on her head.

It's a long evening, and an emotionally draining one. But by the end of it, we're all talked-out and weary, slouched in comfortable silence in the living room. I'm pretty sure this moment is the closest we've come to feeling like a family for longer than I can begin to remember.

BEYOND CRAZY

The past two weeks have totally wiped me out. But on Monday I really need to visit Nana again, and I'm trying my best to psych myself up for that.

I never know what to expect, from one Monday to the next. I'm almost afraid that her room will be empty, her suitcase will be gone. One day I'll show up and they'll say to me 'Your Nana? What was her name again?'

I practically have to force myself through the bus doors when I reach my stop. It's a slow walk along the pathway leading to the front doors of the home. I drag my feet, stare at the ground. And look up when I'm almost at the entrance where there's a couple of park benches. Who's sitting there but Nana, wearing jeans and a blouse, and slippers, as usual. She's eating wine gums.

"Care for a wine gum, honey?" Nana says, offering me the bag.

I take her by the elbow and lead her inside, grinning the entire time. Yes, today I'm doing it, approaching the activity coordinator with my idea about staying around to chill with the other residents on Mondays. *And* about bringing live music into this place. It might help these people feel a little more alive themselves. Not so sure what my bandmates will think of my idea, but I'll be finding that out soon enough.

"How's Nana?" Mom asks me the instant I step inside. There's a cup on the coffee table. That's a good sign. She pats the sofa seat and

I go over to sit beside her. "And how are *you*, Stelle?" she adds, looking straight into my eyes.

"I'm okay, I guess. And so is Nana. Up to her usual tricks." I sprawl against the armrest and tell her about how Nana was sitting there munching on stolen candy. She grins a bit, even chuckles.

Then I mention my plan for taking music into the home, a perfect way to tie my drumming and music passion into my volunteer work. And maybe even make those people's lives a little livelier. And how the director of the home, who plays guitar herself for them now and again, agreed that weekly music nights would be a fine addition. Mom sighs, swallows hard.

"That sounds like a great idea, Stelle. I'm going to try and go over there with you one of these days. I really am. I promise."

"Okay, Mom. Just let me know when you're ready."

She squeezes my arm and half-smiles, and

I almost think I can believe that she really wants to do this.

"You know what else? I think I'm gonna get all my hair cut off. And rock my grey. Have you seen Annie Lennox lately? Short grey hair. She's always been my idol. Still is. And when I start to feel better, I'm going to look into going back to work. I miss being in a library."

"That is an awesome idea." I hug her hard. "*You* are awesome!"

"Huh, I wish." Then my mom clears her throat. "Okay, so I also have a confession to make, Stelle." She digs behind the sofa cushion and slowly pulls something out.

"My cell phone, Mom? Where was it?"

She sets it in my hand. "I hid it under my mattress. God, I'm so sorry. You were always texting people, phoning your friends. Having fun. I guess I resented it or something. It's like I needed to take it away from you. Does that make any sense?"

"I hardly missed it, Mom. And it doesn't

matter now anyway." I hug her arm and lay my head on her shoulder. "You were sick, but now you're going to get better."

———

Later, when I'm in my room trying to make some headway on the English assignment, there's a knock at the door. I bolt from my desk, a bit too glad for the distraction.

"I'll get it," I call to my mom, who's reading on the sofa, still tuned in to MuchRetro. That's got to be another good sign. And Stan's supposedly at the library helping Camilla out with math. Hope that's the truth.

When I open the door, Lu is standing there. Her face is all blotchy and wet.

"What's wrong? What happened?"

Lu sinks onto the top step and pulls on my arm. "Sit. Just listen to this, okay? It's freakin' unbelievable."

I sit. And listen. And can hardly believe what I'm hearing. Or can I?

"So this afternoon my dad is out driving somewhere and he's speeding. He drives fast sometimes. And he gets pulled over." Lu starts gulping air. "And . . . he gets *busted*! For drinking and driving. There'll be lawyers, and probably a trial. What if he has to go to *jail*? He lost his driver's licence for three months as it is."

"Oh crap, Lulu. That totally sucks. Everyone can make mistakes though, right?" I hug her hard.

"I guess so, but my mom is flipping out, and yelling constantly. She says she's leaving him if he doesn't get his act together and stop drinking so much. I'm really scared that she means it this time." Lu heaves a huge sigh, leans in and rests her head on my shoulder.

"You mean it's happened before?" I ask her softly. "The drinking and driving?"

"Of course it has. They always fight about it. Dad says he's going to change. Now that he's been arrested and charged, he has no choice. I've just been too ashamed to talk about it before, I guess."

I rub her back and she wriggles in closer. We both sit there and stare into the thickening October darkness. Lu drones on about her parents, how they love their 'cocktails' after work. If they start bickering, Lu just walks away. It's a part of who they are, she says. Even though she doesn't totally agree with their habits, she tries not to judge them for it. And hopes things will change for the good some day.

Wow. I guess we've all got skeletons hiding in our closets. Just when you think you have the most messed up family on the planet, you find out the dirt on everyone else's. It's beyond crazy, really. I guess nobody ever gets out unscathed when it comes to life and love.

21

BE GENTLE WITH YOURSELF

By the time the bell rings after school on Wednesday, I can't wait to surprise my friends with the new song I've been practicing. I'm doing this, even though I'm not the best singer around. I adjust my drum kit, while Nat and Lu tune up their guitars. Karim sits grinning in his usual spot, his instruments set out on the work bench in front of him.

"Ready to get this party started?" Lu says and he shakes his tambourine.

"Let's do this, ladies!" he says.

"One sec. Can I sing something for you?

No accompaniment needed."

They're all staring at me.

"Wow. Sure, go for it," Lu tells me.

And I do. Because if feels as if I've known this melody forever.

Be Gentle with Yourself

*I just can't seem to make a choice / that
doesn't hit a wall,
And every time I use my voice / I take another
fall.*

*It doesn't matter what I say, I seem to blow it
every day,
It doesn't matter what I do, I'm sure to mess it
up, it's true.*

*And then you go and tell me:
Be gentle with yourself,
Blow away the dust and
Take your feelings off the shelf,*

And so I've opened up my mind / and opened

up the door,
I promise that I'll never hide / my feelings any-
more.

And if I listen with my heart, it's sure to be a
better start,
And if I feel with my soul, it's sure to make me
feel whole . . .

Take a breath, take a chance,
Don't give despair another glance,
Just do your best,
Be gentle with yourself.

When I'm done, there's a stunned silence, until Karim walks over and starts hugging me. And Lu and Nat are right behind him.

Then, instead of a band practice, it turns into something like a group therapy session. We all start pouring out our family angst to each other, sharing all the difficult things that play a part in all of our lives. The ones that are inevitable if you let yourself love people enough.

Lu shares what's happened with her dad's misadventure and how he's lost his driver's licence. I share what's happened with my mom's breakdown and poor old Nana. Nat confesses how hard it is to march to a different drummer and keep believing in yourself.

Karim nods. "Yeah, my mom keeps pushing me to try and be more 'manly' like my dad, even though she has no clue what she's talking about. Like how I act is something I can adjust. And that's not happening *anywhere* in the near future either."

Then Karim tells Nat about his unsupportive family, and the whole toolbox story, which still completely shocks me. But this time, when he tells it, he actually manages to make it sound hilarious.

"I guess we all have mind-numbing family issues, don't we?" Lu says and playfully punches me in the shoulder.

This is the opening I need. To tell them about the first gig I've arranged for *Virago*.

"So, you guys, guess what. I think I got us our very first gig," I tell them and three heads turn to face me, eyebrows raised. "It's . . ." Dare I even say it out loud? "It's at the seniors' home where my Nana lives."

Their faces all register the same look of horror. Then they start laughing like crazy, until they realize I'm not joining them.

"Beatles' songs, some easy folk rock, Neil Young, some Eagles maybe," I tell them, and they stop laughing. "That's the sort of stuff they want."

"You're serious," Lu says.

I nod and shrug. "Gotta start somewhere, don't we, Viragos?"

"Okay, got the first song we can cover!" Karim pipes up. "It's a no-brainer! 'When I'm Sixty-Four'!"

And that's when we all start to laugh.

Drum roll for Saturday, please.

"Do I look okay?" Mom is staring at herself in the mirror on Saturday morning. She hasn't done that in ages.

"You look fine, Mom. Honest. Your jeans are even looser now, have you noticed that?"

"You bet." She's looking at her reflection with something like curiosity. "And I haven't worn this top for a couple of years. It was way too tight on my boobs. Ugh. I've got the middle-aged droops."

"Yikes! Thanks for *that* picture!" I catch her eye in the mirror and pretend to cringe. She offers a vague smile before her face turns solemn.

Did I say too much? Maybe she's not ready for humour yet. How will I ever get all this figured out? Then my mom puts a hand on my arm. When our eyes meet, she has a funny look on her face.

"What's it like playing the drums, anyway, Stelle?" she says. "I always thought I might like to play them back when I was your age."

"Seriously?" My face explodes into a smile. "Hey, you can try mine out any old time you want to. It's great for beating out your angst."

"Can't wait to give it a shot," Mom says, almost smiling.

Mom's a little nervous today. She hasn't willingly left the house in I can't remember how long. But she wants to come to our band practice at Lu's place — amazing! When I mentioned it, she said she needed to find something decent to wear. So I helped her find something decent to wear.

I've invited Dad and Josie, too, since they have to listen to all the pounding in their basement all the time. Mom said she's okay with it. Stan might drop by with Camilla. I'm sure Lu's parents, Xing and Peter, will be there too, if they're talking to each other, that is. Nat is bringing her mom along to prove to her that it doesn't always have to be about math. Karim figures he should wait a while before he breaks the news to his family that he's in a band now.

Virago has been rehearsing for this moment all week. Even though there's a guy in the band, he's most definitely 'warlike' and 'heroic'. We all are.

Every night after school we've been meeting at Lu's to practice the song. *Be Gentle with Yourself.* Which I'm dedicating to my mom, the original Virago Girl.